PRAISE FOR EDWARD BUNKER

'...nker is among the tiny band of American
...ters whose work possesses integrity, crafts-
...d moral passion ... an artist with a unique
...ing voice.'
William Styron

'...see why Bunker has acquired such diverse
...Quentin Tarantino and William Styron ...
...guishes Bunker from other crime writers is
... convey the compassion dormant within his
...inals without resorting to excess luridness,
...moralism.'
Publishers Weekly

'...ker writes about the netherworld of society's
... a passion and insight that comes from hav-
...close to the bone.'
The Los Angeles Times

'...ts straight – his direct and transparent prose
...'primacy of violence' that defines life in the
Kirkus Reviews

'...ker is a true original of American letters. His
...minal classics: novels about criminals, writ-
...criminal, from the unregenerately criminal
James Ellroy

'The most compelling quality of *No Beast So Fierce* is that, solidly rooted in his own experiences, it explores the nature of the criminal mind with almost blinding authenticity. Bunker is obviously a man of unusual gifts honed under circumstances that would destroy most men'

Los Angeles Times

'Quite simply, one of the great crime novels of the past 30 years' James Ellroy

'Hard as Nails' *Loaded*

'The best first person crime novel I have ever read' Quentin Tarantino

'(*No Beast So Fierce*) is a gripping and harrowing read' *Daily Mail*

'*The Animal Factory* joins Solzhenitsyn's *One Day in the Life of Ivan Denisovich* and George Jackson's *Soledad Brother* in the front rank of prison literature – a stone classic.'

Time Out

'(*Little Boy Blue*) is a scalding experience – and a literary triumph in the tradition of Dreiser, Farrell and James Jones. This is an important book.' Roderick Thorp

'(*Dog Eat Dog*) is the 'angel dust' of crime fiction: thrillingly violent and addictive, surging with exhilaration and fear' *The Evening Standard*

Also by the same author

No Beast so Fierce
The Animal Factory
Little Boy Blue
Dog Eat Dog
Mr Blue

Edward Bunker will be back with his final book –

DEATH ROW BREAKOUT

– in 2009. Read a story from this book online now at
www.noexit.co.uk/deathrowbreakout

EDWARD BUNKER

stark

FOREWORD BY JAMES ELLROY
AFTERWORD BY JENNIFER STEELE

no exit press

This edition published in 2008 by No Exit Press,
P.O.Box 394, Harpenden, Herts, AL5 1XJ
www.noexit.co.uk

A CIP catalogue record for this book is available from the British Library.

EAN 978-1-84243-264-8

2 4 6 8 10 9 7 5 3 1

Typeset by Ellipsis Books Limited, Glasgow
Printed and bound in Great Britain by
J.H. Haynes & Co Ltd., Sparkford, Yeovil, Somerset

For
Brendan Bunker

Foreword

Edward Bunker wrote journalistic pieces, short fiction and novels in and out of prison. His first efforts are reform-school newsletter entries circa 1950. Those pieces cannot be found today. Several early novel manuscripts written during Mr. Bunker's San Quentin jolts cannot be found. The short novel, *Stark*, apparently of late-60s/early-70s vintage, was discovered after Mr. Bunker's 2005 death.

It's thus a period book within a period book. Set in the early 60s in a Southern California beach town, it's a wiiiiiild hybrid of 50s paperback-original pulp/noir and punk's fantasy. It's a prophecy of the fine writer Mr. Bunker would become.

The title character is a hophead and a grifter out to fill his pockets with gelt – and fill his arm with big "H". He's run afoul of the fuzz. He's out to screw the squarejohn world. He craves boss threads, fast rides, slick bitches. He's bopping through the world of the quadruple cross. He's hip. He's so cool he's freon frigid. He's fatuously fatalistic. He knows it's avant garde to assume your own doom. He's trying to kill his way through a maze of pissed-off lowlifes and beat the green room at Big Q, laboring under parole restrictions and a heroin habit. It's the creation of a young convict torqued on raisinjack, Mickey Spillane and frog existentialism – and it all works in the end.

It's kid-writer stuff that Eddie Bunker fans should dig on. It would have made the grade as a Fawcett Gold Medal paperback original back in the 50s along with the work of John D. McDonald and Kurt Vonnegut. Read it. It will make you want to turn tricks and geez dope. I'm jonesing for some "Horse" right now. Fatalism is far-out. Hey, Big Dead Eddie – I grok your groove, Daddy-o!

James Ellroy

Stark

1

Ernie Stark was not the nicest guy you'd ever meet. Ask his friends. If he had any. He was a two-bit hustler who dreamt that the next score would be the big one. The one that would put him on easy street. But too often, he was outsmarted. If not by the sucker, then by the law.

Look at the latest situation he was in. Because of a stupid bust while he was still on parole, he was in bed with the cops. Stark had done a lot of shady things, but being a rat, a stool pigeon for the cops, was not a role he enjoyed. It was either that or going back to the slammer. He'd rather be a rat – outside.

The cops knew that his Hawaiian pal, Momo, was a

dealer. Small time stuff. They didn't want him; they wanted his supplier. If they arrested Momo, the next higher up on the drug chain would disappear. They'd even arrest Momo if they knew where his goods were.

So, you hired a rat like Stark to get close to his pal and get the name of the supplier of Momo's drugs. Easier said than done, mused Stark, sitting at the bar next to Momo in their favorite nightclub. It was 1962, and the Panama was the best popular club in Oceanview.

Complicating things for Stark was that he was slowly getting hooked on heroin. Shit that his pal Momo was supplying at cut-rate prices to his buddy. He wasn't hooked yet, but he was getting there. It was what had got him in this spot with the cops. He now had a twice-a-day habit. He had a growing monkey on his back.

He also had to keep an eye on Dummy, a mute who everyone had avoided in the joint. He and Dummy had been in prison together. He for a bunko caper that went bad, Dummy for manslaughter. No con ever touched Dummy, after the one who tried to get too friendly and later wound up dead. Stark had even learned some basic phrases to sign to Dummy, but the guy read lips. You soon learned never to kid him – to his face.

Dummy hung around the club, watching things. He had some sort of a deal with Momo. Stark guessed he was a runner. Maybe he could lead him to the Man?

Stark looked at his watch. He was late. Crowley would be pissed. Fuck him. How was he going to make his meet, with Dummy watching his every move? Dummy was no friend. He almost never smiled. And when he did, some-body died.

"I gotta see a guy," he told Momo. "I'll be back in a few minutes. Save my seat." Momo didn't reply. He just waved him off. He didn't expect a farewell pat from Dummy.

2

Detective Lieutenant Patrick Crowley sat in the shad-owed darkness of the unmarked police car. The street was squalid, lined with third-rate rooming houses. The neighborhood was the heart of Oceanview's tender-loin. From where he sat, Crowley could see across the street the side door of the Panama Club, the doorway illu-minated by a moth-haloed electric bulb. Crowley could see the action coming and going and hear faintly the sound of a jukebox repeating the same blues number over and over. The clarity of the music swelled and eddied in proportion to the other sounds carried by the night air; the burst of crude laughter, the whiskey-thickened voices rising in a gust of excitement. A yellow streetcar grumbled past, its bell ringing dully. A taxi paused to pick up a fare and disappeared into elsewhere.

Crowley glanced at his wristwatch and his heavy lips formed a silent curse. He shook his head and again watched the doorway, unable to hold back a grin as a known prostitute steered out a trick to some cheap room. Crowley wasn't interested in stopping vice. He was a narcotics cop. He was waiting for his rat.

The side door opened again and from it stepped a slender man in expensive sports clothes. A cigarette lighter flared in his hand. A moment later the headlights of the police car flashed for a second. The man finished lighting the cigarette and leisurely crossed the street. Crowley grunted in disgust and started the motor. It was Stark.

Stark's eyes flicked up and down the street, into shadows and over his shoulder, but his movements were casual. He walked with one hand draped in a jacket pocket, the other with the cigarette swung in loose exaggeration at his side. He was tall, with slightly stooped shoulders and a certain feline grace, a hip swagger halfway between poise and a pose. He knew he was good-looking in an ascetic kind of way. He'd seen Humphrey Bogart walk this way in a movie. He came around the car and slipped through the passenger door. Slamming it closed behind himself, he extended his left arm along the back of the seat and leaned back in the corner.

Crowley was already spinning the car into an illegal U-turn. Stark looked at the overweight bulk behind the wheel and mused that seventeen years on the force had made Pat Crowley more a cop than the television stereotype.

When they were beyond the city limits, Stark made a face of pain.

"Man, couldn't you have been cooler?" he asked. "Maybe parked down the street or something? If anybody saw me with you, my ass is grass. I live down here, and I don't dig the idea of getting my throat cut. There's suckers that do things like that."

"You've been stalling," Crowley said. "I get tired of waiting for your games. You were supposed to call me today. You didn't, so I came for you. What've you got for me?"

"It ain't as easy as you think, Pat."

The detective turned his eyes from the highway to glare at Stark. "We're not on a first name basis, punk."

"Just trying to be friendly."

"We're not friends. This is business. We made a deal that you begged for… I wouldn't press charges for the junk I found in your pocket, and you'd set up the big connection. You promised – I went for it. I'll even take Mr. Momo Mendoza. He's just one step over you. He might give up his supplier, if I could nail him with enough shit to put him away for twenty years."

"I'll get him, but I can't if you crowd me. Just leave me to handle it."

"You made the deal, but I make the rules. When I want you, you come. Otherwise you'll talk to me from a cell.

You won't like going cold turkey. I've seen what it does to punks like you."

"Okay, man." Stark looked to the whirring scenery, the moon-silvered ocean rushing up the beach to break in foamy blue froth, mist filling the night with the smell of the sea. He cursed himself for his recklessness in taking a shot of the Beast from the East in the toilet of a gas station. The attendant had become suspicious and called the police, and when Stark came out, Lieutenant Pat Crowley was waiting. He hadn't known that the toilet had become a favorite shooting gallery.

That had been a week ago. Now the pressure was on. He had tried to ignore his agreement with Crowley. In fact, he didn't know how he was going to deliver. Momo was very secretive about his connection. Deadly secretive. He was also his pal and his connection. How the fuck did he ever get trapped into this deal? Momo never had his goods on him. He always went somewhere to get the customer's order.

"Man," Stark said, "this ain't the supermarket. Momo's not a fool. I can't just ask him who his connection is. If I get too nosy, he'll freeze me out. You've been in the game long enough to know the junkie world is paranoid. Nobody trusts anybody."

"They shouldn't. You're all finks. I might as well lock you up, pinch Momo, and let him set up the big man. Find out where Momo hides his shit. We've already been through his place once."

Stark kept silent. He knew that Momo was no fink.

He'd go to prison first. It wouldn't bother him. It was the price you paid for his kind of business.

"I want some results," Crowley said. "If it was up to me, I'd lock you up. You think you're slick, Stark, too goddamn slick for the world."

"Well, *you're* not slick," he replied petulantly, "calling the Panama Club and making me meet you outside."

"Keep your appointments."

"I couldn't."

"Some whore…"

Stark didn't answer. His jaw was set tight with futile resentment. "What do you want me to do now?"

"The same. Get next to Momo's boss. Tell Momo you want to make some big money or some other story. You're good at stories. Get to work on it. You have two days to come through. If something doesn't happen by then, I'll pick you up and turn the key."

"Okay, okay. I got it. I'm working on an angle. I think the key guy may be Dummy, the mute. The guy's a killer. Did you ever see his eyes? He scares me."

"Bullshit. You got two days. Now fuck off."

Stark exited the police car two blocks from the Panama Club. He stood in the thickening fog and watched the red taillights turn out of sight. His eyes gleamed with anger; his lean face twisted. He spat with fury, as if cleansing his mouth of filth.

"Big, tough cop," he snarled. Suddenly the ugliness became laughter. Using two fingers of his left hand scissor-like, he fished a shriveled marijuana cigarette from a shirt pocket. "Yeah, copper, I had a felony in my pocket. You think you've got me, but I've got the whole world. All you hoosiers, suckers, coppers. Screw you. Screw Momo. And screw Mr. Big, whoever the fool is."

A clock in the window of a cut-rate jewelry store gave the time as a few minutes past midnight. There was no hurry; the club stayed open until two.

Stark pinched free the twisted end of the cigarette, ran it over his tongue to dampen the paper, lit it, sucking deeply, and began to walk down the deserted street.

He wondered if pot could still give him the ride. The stick of grass had been a gift from the bartender. Stark hadn't wanted it at the time, but didn't want to offend the guy, who thought marijuana was the best kick in the world. His own attitude had been prejudiced long ago by a dope fiend, his pool-hustler father, the fast man who said: "I don't need shitty weed to make me crazier. Man, I need God's medicine to make me sane." And then busted the vein with a needle while his son watched. His father had been a junkie. Stark vowed he'd never get hooked. Only suckers got hooked.

He dragged once more on the joint, and as he held his breath this time, the marijuana worked its magic. In seconds his mind zoomed to a higher level of perspective, at once more intense and yet distorted. Crowley's face came to mind, bulldog and stupid. A sudden fit of laughter erupted. His laughter booming through the silence of the empty streets. He checked himself, aware that the grass was playing with his imagination. The lights were brighter, and the windows that had been ugly moments before seemed like rows of impressionist paintings hung by a great artist in the gallery of night. The thought brought another gust of insane laughter.

Trash cans, battered by use, lined the curbs, waiting for dawn. These, too, had meaning, especially a deformed washtub heaped to overflow by wine bottles. Stark stopped abruptly, leaned far forward and narrowed his bloodshot eyes.

"I'll be goddamned," he said in solemn awe. "It's a bloody avant garde masterpiece..." He laughed at his own ridiculousness.

A black and white prowl car slid to the curb, its bright headlights bathing him. It immediately broke his mood. A policeman, featureless beneath the bill of his hat, popped his head from the window, like a puppet from a box.

"What're ya doin' out here, buddy? It's late to be roaming."

"Just digging the crazy art."

"What?"

"Bringing out the rubbish." He knew the officer had stopped to see if he was a drunk. The hustler straightened himself. "They pick it up early. I work nights so I brought it out. Glad to see you on the job. It makes me feel safer leaving my wife home alone."

"Okay, mister. Don't work too hard." He looked pointedly down at the numerous wine bottles. "And watch your ulcers."

The police car slid away to prowl other places in the night. Stark watched it and sobered up. "Better be cool before this happy grass gets me locked up for laughing at the moon."

He quickened his pace toward the Panama Club.

3

Sounds of strident jukebox saxophone reached out to Stark as he neared the door of the Panama Club. A marine staggered out, shirt unbuttoned and hat askew, and stood wavering on the sidewalk as if debating which course his life should take. He was one of numberless servicemen who came from as far away as San Diego in search of liquor, laughter, and a lay.

Stark detoured around the drunk and slipped inside. Blatant light, screaming percussion, and the odor of cigarette and perfume assaulted his senses simultaneously. He loved it all. It was his turf. He stood in the shadows while his eyes adjusted to the glare. He scanned the large, pulsating room – bar, small dance floor, the filled tables, crowded, though not as jammed as on weekends. Rock and roll boomed from the jukebox. A bleached B-girl and a rosy cheeked sailor were the only dancers.

Through the haze and movement, Stark saw Momo and Dummy at the far end of the bar, just where he'd left them. Dummy was sharply dressed as always, wearing a salt and pepper sports coat. His handsome face was unlined. Momo was just the opposite. He was hulking, drab, unpressed; as soon as he put on clothes his blobbish figure wrinkled them. His face was swarthy, pockmarked, and shiny with sweat. What a pair, he thought.

Stark moved smoothly between the tables, skirted the dance floor, nodded a hip hello to the barmaid, and arrived behind the two men.

"A little air," he said to Momo, nodding to Dummy. Stark slipped between them, glancing at the profile of Momo Mendoza's swarthy, acne-pitted face.

"Where'd you go?" Momo asked. "You've been gone a while."

Before Stark could reply Dummy demanded attention in the hand language of mutes. He pointed to Stark's head and made a motion as if turning on a faucet. The implication was clear. Stark grinned and winked, relieved.

Dummy nodded. He patted the lean-faced man on the shoulder, took a quarter from the stack of coins on the bar, and moved away. Stark turned once more to Momo.

"Where'd you go?" the Hawaiian repeated. "Somebody said they saw you get in a car."

Stark was stunned. Dummy must have spotted him. He cut his eyes to Momo's black, expressionless pools and momentarily could not think. Instantly, he gained control of himself, but wondered if Momo suspected or had seen his reaction. He leaned toward the man in a ludicrous exaggeration of conspiracy: "Man," he whispered, "that was Harry Anstetter, chief of the whole damn state narcotics bureau."

Momo's face cracked into a slight smile at the ridiculousness. A smile was not enough. Stark leaned closer, his mouth almost touching Momo's ear.

"Don't tell anybody, keep it cool, but old Harry didn't come on business. The guy's an undercover pansy… been in love with me for years."

Momo's smile grew to vulgar laughter, Stark's fear dissipating with the sound of it. He flagged a bartender and ordered a glass of ginger ale. While waiting for it, he said off-handedly that he had gone to smoke some marijuana that a friend had given him.

"I didn't think you liked pot," Momo said.

"Now and then… I go for anything. He's been bugging me to get some. Hell, that was my drug of choice, until you started giving me free rides of your shit. Now I got to have a couple of tastes every day. Like medicine. One in the a.m. and one in the p.m."

Momo nudged him and gestured with a thumb toward the jukebox. Dummy had slipped there, leaning into the vibrations of the music. It was one of the rare times he saw Dummy smile. Stark snickered, but was not interested;

more important things were on his mind:

"You got anything for my p.m.?"

"It'll cost you a ten spot. And that's my wholesale price."

"I've got the dough. You got a couple of bundles?"

"Not here. It's near my pad. It won't take long to get to."

"At your bargain prices, I should take a couple days' worth."

Momo nodded. "How soon do you need it? The club closes in another hour."

"The sooner the better. This weed's got my brain fuzzy as the jute mill in San Quentin."

Momo nodded his head again, this time sympathetically. "Marijuana is for sex freaks. I don't mess with it myself." He lifted a shot glass of cheap bar whiskey and dumped it down his throat. On the way out, Momo paused at the jukebox to wave to Dummy. The mute nodded goodbye and stared at Stark, his eyes never leaving the two as they departed.

On the street outside, followed by the strains of music and surrounded by a light fog, Stark said, "Dummy makes me nervous. His eyes are scary. Even in the joint guys avoided him. He's cold, man. You'd think after our doing time together he'd be friendlier."

"He's okay," Momo said. "He's reliable. And people don't fuck with him. A little crazy, maybe. But reliable."

"Does he work for you? How does he make his dough? Is he a stickup artist?"

Momo ignored his questions, but smiled. "The dames seem to find him attractive."

Both men grinned sardonically and entered the parking lot where Stark's six-year-old Chevy wagon was parked. The vehicle was the remnant of his brief employment by a Los Angeles vending machine company. They'd provided the wreck. He kept it when they split. He'd had a nice little side racket going, before the cops nabbed him. He'd been skimming the machines and competing with them by selling owners and bartenders untaxed butts he brought in from Mexico. He hadn't bargained on being caught by the cops before the Mob noticed a drop-off in sales. He was lucky that all he got was two years in the slammer and three years parole. It was not his first offense. Earlier, another foolproof scam had gone wrong, and he'd been caught. He was twenty-eight years old and had a total of five years in jail – including his juvie stretch. That was three years ago. A lifetime back.

The ride to Momo's dump was brief and quiet. On the way, Stark found himself remembering a story he'd heard about Dummy. Seems like the first time he got busted, he and another kid had tried to hold up a gas station. The other kid was underage, Dummy was eighteen. When the attendant refused to open the cash register, Dummy made noises, which made the guy laugh, despite the gun Dummy was holding. "Go on home and give your pa his gun," the guy cracked. This made Dummy mad, and he hit him on the side of his head with the gun, which went off. The two would-be robbers ran off with nothing. The attendant identified the kid, who lived in the neighbor-hood. The kid gave up Dummy. The kid went to juvenile hall, and Dummy went to prison. It was later reported that shortly after Dummy got out of prison, the kid was found stabbed to death.

And Crowley expects me to rat out this guy? Better Momo, a pal, than that killer.

At Momo's address the two men went quickly up the creaking stairs and down the dreary hallway, lit only by a bare lightbulb dangling from the ceiling. Momo turned his key in the lock and nudged the door open.

"Wait inside," he said, "I'll go get the stash."

"Make it quick, sport. I wanna geeze."

"Just a few minutes. Make yourself comfortable."

Momo went back down the hall. Stark heard the creak of stairs and moved into the apartment. It was one dark room with a bathroom and kitchenette. The only light was the wan rectangle from the hallway where he stood. It splashed out over a double bed. Stark was instantly aware that someone was sleeping in it. A glance around showed a dame's clothes on the back of a chair. A foot, with carmine toenails, protruded from the mounds of sheets and blankets.

When Stark shut the door and found the light switch, the sleeper shifted around, face still hidden.

"Is that you, baby?" asked a husky voice.

"It's me, baby, whoever I am. But am I the baby you're talking about?"

The girl swam above the blankets, rubbing her eyes

from sleep. When she stopped rubbing them, he could see her beautiful emerald eyes with their telltale pinpoint pupils.

"Who the fuck are you? How'd you get in?"

"Name's Stark. Friend and associate of Momo. Sorry about waking you up. He just let me in. He's gone to get something I need."

"That's no big thing. Traffic's heavy here." She reached for a pack of cigarettes on a cluttered nightstand, found it empty, and with a sigh threw it, crumpled, onto an overflowing ashtray.

Silently Stark lit two cigarettes and handed her one. He wondered what this good-looking dame was doing, shacked up in a dump with a grub like Momo. If she was hooked, she was pretty enough to work as a call girl in the big leagues of the Apple or Hollywood.

"Have you got a name?" he asked, "or do I just call you 'pretty'?"

"Call me pretty by all means, but Dorie Williams is my name." She smiled. It lit up her entire face, especially those green eyes flecked with gold. For a brief moment she was a bright little girl with auburn hair and traces of freckles across her unpowdered nose. "And your name is... I forgot?"

"Stark."

"Stark. That's neat. Man of few words. I like that."

"Action speaks louder than words. That's me."

Stark sat down in a straight-backed chair and tilted it back against the wall, stretching out his long legs. Dorie dragged on her cigarette and let the smoke curl from her wide mouth into her nostrils.

"Where's Momo?"

"He went down the hall. He's taking care of business."

Dorie nodded. She was wide awake now and moved back against the headboard, her knees up, still covered to her neck by the sheet. She watched him closely, studying.

"How do I know you're not a burglar or a rapo?"

"You can't. I'm too smart to be a burglar, that's not my racket. And as for being a rapo, why steal what's available for sale?"

Dorie blushed for a moment, then threw back her head and laughed. "You talk just like Humphrey Bogart. I've only known you five minutes, and you think I'm for sale. That's pretty cold," she said, her voice mocking.

"You might call me that."

They were momentarily silent, appraising each other. Dorie moved to mash out the cigarette and the sheet slipped away from her breasts, exposing full brownish-nippled whiteness. He wondered if the flash was on purpose.

"Where'd Momo find you?" Dorie asked.

"Find me?"

"Yeah, find you? Locate you? Meet you? Catch you?"

"You mean, he's never mentioned my name? We're old friends. I've just been away for a while."

"Away? Prison? A guy like you? Too smart to be a burglar?"

"Hey, everyone makes mistakes. Even you. How'd you

STARK

hook up with Momo? And why?"

"Same as you. Shooting up and going to hell. It's as good a place as any. But for your information, Momo found me in a nuthouse."

"I was going to guess that. Camarillo?"

"Yes."

"You were taking a cure?"

"That and recuperating from a nervous breakdown. They fixed the last but not the first."

"How long were you there?"

"Six months. It was a self-commitment."

"And Momo was there to beat a felony charge. Now back in the twilight zone."

"Yep. I'm what you might call real friendly with my connection. And it's a ball. Real choice."

"Whatever you like for kicks, I guess."

"I like to try everything once."

Stark fell silent, eyes flitting to the door, ears tuned for the first sound of Momo's approaching steps.

"He should be back by now," Dorie said. "It doesn't usually take him that long."

"Maybe he got busted. What'll you do then?"

She shrugged. "You look promising… for a while."

The statement was scarcely out of her mouth when the door knob turned. Dorie pulled the sheets up as Momo slipped in and fastened the nightchain.

"Sorry to hang you up," he said. "It took a little longer than usual to get your order."

"Where did you go?" asked Stark.

33

"The less you know the better."

Stark grinned. "Cool by me. Can I fix here?"

"I guess it's okay. I'm gonna fix myself. What about you, Dorie?"

"Never leave me out of that automobile ride, honey. I love it."

Momo led them to the bathroom. He handed Stark one of the toy red balloons. They were tied at the top, making tiny asymmetrical balls. Within each was ten capsules of shit.

"Get the outfit, baby," Momo commanded Dorie. Then he extended his hand palm upward to Stark. "That'll be forty bucks for the bindles."

"You're sure a trusting soul," Stark said, as he slipped him a few bills.

Momo grabbed the bills and stuffed them in his pocket, uncounted, in his impatience to get fixed. He stepped to the doorway, looking at Dorie. She was on the far side of the room, standing tiptoe on a chair by the front door, probing with eager fingers in a crevice of the moulding overhead.

"You gonna take all night to get the goddamn outfit?" Momo asked.

"It's wedged in, honey. Be cool and I'll have it in a second."

Momo grunted unintelligibly and waited, watching her. She didn't seem to be making progress. The sight of her ass trembling through her sheer negligee as she struggled somehow increased his impatience. He was moving forward to get it himself when she turned.

"Here it is," she said. She came lithely down from the chair, extending the outfit. He took it wordlessly and spun back to the tiny bathroom.

Stark was beside the sink. He had taken the spoon from the medicine cabinet and it lay on the yellowed porcelain. In the spoon was white powder.

"Let me have it." Stark said.

"Have what?" Momo asked.

"The fit." He gestured to the spread-out paraphernalia. "I'm ready and I'm in a hurry. Let me go first."

Momo looked at the spoon and shook his head incredulously. "You've got balls. This is my pad. I fix first. Ain't that right, baby?"

Dorie smiled enigmatically and shrugged. She wouldn't take sides.

"What the hell are you trying to pull?" Momo flared.

"Shouldn't a good host let a guest, a paying guest, go first?" said Stark.

Momo's face flushed. His jaws flexed and his lips pressed tightly. He did not like Stark's thinly veiled sarcasm.

"Are ya lookin' for a trip to the hospital?" Momo asked. He leaned forward in a challenge.

Stark saw the danger and shifted gears. He grinned widely and slapped Momo on the shoulder. "Man, don't get me wrong. I'm not trying to pull a fast one, and I don't want to hassle with you. You're my pal... and the best connection in town. And you ain't no chump. I know

that. It's just that I'm in a hurry, got things on my mind."
He spoke fast, joshingly, with seeming sincerity.

Momo's face softened. He looked down. "Okay, man,
let it go. Forget it. I just lost my temper for a second."

"You ought to apologize for threatening your friends,"
Stark chided. "Instead, let me fix first and then I'll know
you're sorry."

Momo froze, blinked, and then guffawed. He waved a
hand toward the sink. "Be my guest." He turned to Dorie,
who had watched intently. "This guy could sell chastity
belts to prostitutes. But I like him, the bastard."

"Yes, I know. He's attractive, in a dumb kind of way. A
real hustler."

Stark brushed Dorie with a sharp glance. She had made
several strange remarks in the brief minutes since he met
her. She had a weird quickness of mind he liked but that
could be dangerous. He would have to watch her, but
damn it if she didn't have his number.

"Do me a favor, baby," he said. "Get me something to
tie off with."

"An old nylon of mine. How's that?" Her eyebrows
raised in mock coquettishness and her voice was affectedly
husky, a little Veronica Lake. She, too, was a blonde.

"That'll do it," he said. He ignored the gambit.

Momo was too preoccupied in unwrapping the
makeshift hypodermic kit to notice the exchange. He
placed the needle and eyedropper next to the spoon, and
then half filled a glass with water.

"Make it quick," he said. "I'm next."

Stark ignored both Momo and Dorie. She left the bathroom to fetch the nylon. The shapely dame moved with the swift sureness of a priest performing a grotesque ritual. The needle was fitted onto the eyedropper, the tip of which was wrapped in black thread. Water was sucked from the glass through the needle to make sure it would not clog. A much smaller amount of water was drained into the powder-filled spoon. Several matches were lit simultaneously, the scent of burning sulphur rising up to churn Stark's stomach with nausea. The spoon was moved over the flame and the powder dissolved, becoming a steamy clear liquid tinted faintly brown.

Stark carefully placed the spoon on the sink and picked up a tiny piece of cotton. He rolled it between thumb and forefinger into a hard little ball, and dropped it into the bubbling junk. With trembling fingers he pressed the tip of the needle against the cotton and sucked up the liquid. He handed the eyedropper to Momo — whose eyes were glittering black — and shed his coat. Dorie had returned, the stocking stretched chest high between both hands. As Stark finished rolling up his sleeve, she moved forward and wordlessly wrapped the nylon around his left bicep, brushing one of her breasts across the other arm as she leaned over.

"Tighter," he commanded, feeling the blood being trapped. Even in the urgency of the moment he became aware of her warm breath against his cheek, and of her flesh. As she tightened her grip, her unfettered breast beneath the filmy negligee pressed closer against his body.

He knew that this girl, so strange and innocent, so hard and hip, was trying to turn him on. She might think she could manipulate him. He smiled at the idea, for sex had never been his weakness. Shit was his current weakness. There wasn't room for a dame, too.

He forgot Dorie as he tapped the needle into the ridge of vein. A stream of blood filled the eyedropper.

"Here's to J. Edgar Hoover," he said with a smile, and squeezed off the hit.

The glow exploded and suffused him almost instantly. It was a crushing blow that weakened his knees, but sent him to lalaland.

"Nice," he muttered, "Nice. Real nice." The words came out in a guttural monotone. He cleared his throat. "It's good shit, Momo. The best you've ever had. Is this a new brand?"

Momo paused in his own preparations. "It's from a new package I picked up today. The Man said it would be top grade from now on."

"It is," Stark said, face pale and eyelids fluttering. His face was breaking into a sweat. "Real good. Did he say where this new shit came from?"

"No. But you know how connections are – never quit bragging about their stuff."

"This one's right," Stark gasped. "Better be cool. Don't overdose. Maybe you should cut it a bit for other customers." He wavered and felt the nausea rising in his stomach. "I'm gonna sit down, before I fall down. I'll be in the other room."

Momo nodded jerkily without looking up. He was intent on cooking his own fix.

Stark stumbled blindly around Dorie and went to the unmade bed and stretched out in a semi-prone position, back braced by the headboard, head slumping loosely forward to his chest. Through the haze of euphoria he could hear her urging Momo to hurry, the urgent cry of another junkie in need.

Momo would hurry, Stark was certain. He dreamily visualized the fat Hawaiian moving swiftly, the girl hovering impatiently at his shoulder. Momo would hurry, both because he craved the flash and because of Dorie's obvious need to fix. The drug peddler was paying for her flesh with his drugs. A nice setup. Everyone in happy land, Stark thought sardonically.

Stark smiled at the thought of how he might get the info Crowley wanted from the girl. She could wheedle it out of Momo in ten hot seconds of teasing. And he, in turn, would be able, later, to mix business with pleasure as he screwed the information out of her. Anything to get Crowley off his back. He shifted to a more upright position.

"Man, this is serious," he muttered.

"What's serious?" Momo asked. He had finished in the bathroom and stood in the doorway, eyes heavy lidded.

"I was going into a bad nod. That's how people die... just coast on out. I dig the nod, but I'm not ready for the big one."

"Yeah, that would be serious... especially in my pad

where I'd have to get rid of your body." Momo paused, brushed a fluttering hand across his eyes, and smiled. "I'm glad you warned me to take it easy. He wasn't jiving about the stuff. I might've overjolted. I think I'm going to have to cut it for my other customers."

"Yeah, like I told you to. I got other good business ideas. You could use a guy like me. I'm always figuring the odds."

Stark looked at Momo, drowsing on his feet, and decided to try a wild shot in the dark, a direct approach.

"I'd like to meet your connection and make a big buy."

The effect was negative. Momo sneered with arrogance, but without suspicion. He shook his head disdainfully. "Not a chance," he said, moving to an armchair. "But how come you wanna make a big buy all of a sudden?"

"All of a sudden you've got good stuff."

"That don't make no difference. When you score, it's from me. Small buy, big buy, all the same. The Man don't wanna meet nobody."

Stark shrugged. "I was trying to save some money. Sort of your loss is my gain sort of thing. Know what I mean?"

"Yeah, I know. Your style, tryin' to get me to help you take money out of my pocket. You planning to be my competition?"

"No. Your business partner. I got some good ideas."

Momo made a wry face. "Stop it. You're killin' me. But like I said, the Man don't wanna meet nobody. Besides, where'd you get all the dough? If you'd made a big score, I'd a heard about it. You ain't been out long enough."

Stark feigned indifference. "We'll talk about it tomorrow."

"We can talk anytime, but we ain't going anywhere."

Stark tossed a shoulder, sleepily accepting the reply. He hadn't expected anything in the first place. He checked his watch.

"Anyway, I've gotta go. Nothing's happening here." He stood up, unzipped his pants, and tugged his shirt firmly down inside them.

"Hey, baby!" he called toward the bathroom. "I'm splitting."

Dorie appeared, eyes glassy. A tiny spot of blood from the needle puncture was on her left arm. She grabbed Stark's jacket in the other hand. "Don't forget this. What's your hurry? Why don't you just lay back and enjoy the trip?" she said provocatively.

"I've got some business to take care of."

"Monkey business?"

"No. Money business," he said, stepping forward and turning his back to her. "Do you mind?" he asked, extending his arms suggestively.

She snapped the jacket with a flourish and slipped it over his arms.

"So, now the Dark Prince departs."

Stark ignored her, and walked to the door. "See you tomorrow, Momo."

"Anytime after ten. I'll be at the club."

Stark's fingers twisted the knob; then he turned to face them, laughter edging the corners of his mouth. He looked directly at Dorie. "Goodnight, Miss Williams. It's been delightful meeting someone as refined as yourself. And goodnight to you too, Mr. Mendoza, a gentleman and a scholar if ever I met one."

He opened the door slightly and peered out; it was a move conditioned by experience. There was nobody in the dim hallway. Glancing back over his shoulder, he said, "Better lock it. There's all kinds of weird characters around in this neighborhood."

Dorie's face flushed as she stepped forward. "I will double lock it, Mr. Stark." Under her breath, she added: "You bastard."

The door slammed shut behind him, Stark walked toward the stairs, laughing loud enough for her to hear him.

4

The hour was that of the pre-dawn hush, the deathlike period of a city when no human being seems to move, when the headlights of a vehicle add to the sense of aloneness rather than ease it. It was the hour when most who are on the move are either members of the law or those against the law. It was Stark's favorite time of night.

Stark had lied to Momo and Dorie. His only business was a telephone call, and this would be a surprise wake-up call to the person who received it. Beyond that, there was only bed and sleep, both of which he craved. The call would be made from Eric's, an all night coffee shop on the coast highway. It was on a direct line to his small, beachside apartment, the whereabouts of which he kept secret. Nobody could give it up to questioning police if they did not know its location. The less people knew about him, the better he liked it.

His pad would reveal too much. He never invited anyone home. He didn't want anyone to know where he lived. Or how he lived. Some of the furnishings, the books, the glassware had been heisted. He liked to surround himself with beautiful things whether he could afford them or not. His world was shit, inhabited by predators like himself. He came home to escape the jungle. He treasured his privacy after three years in prison.

After a nerve-grinding ride through impenetrable fog, he turned the station wagon into the coffee shop's parking lot. He was not surprised when his headlights played across Dummy's gleaming red Corvette. The mute often came here after the bars closed at two a.m., as did others of the hustler jungle: flashy pimps feeding gaudy whores, insomniac dope fiends (despite drowsy eyes), owl-eyed Benzedrine freaks, thieves with nothing to do who wanted conversation, and a pervert or two seeking a companion for strange embraces. They sat over coffee, smoked endless cigarettes, and cut up the night's deals. Stark knew most of Eric's occupants, at least by face. He also knew that, though he was accepted here, he was not truly one of them. He was beyond their range of bad, a wolf among vultures. He carried, as a part of his being, a deep contempt for them. They were suckers, too, and when the hunting for easier game proved slim, he was not above ripping them off.

He pulled into a vacant slot beside the Corvette. As he got out, he felt compelled to touch the shiny hood. It radiated success. Money. It didn't seem right that a deaf mute interested only in clothes, dope, and sadism should be so successful, while he was just skating by. It wasn't that Dummy made so much more money, it was that he didn't have a monkey on his back. The car and the jukebox seemed to be his only expenses, except for an occasional joint or two.

Stark looked at the Corvette and wondered how Dummy was making his money. He knew better than to ask him. He knew he carried a gun and had used it. Whatever means of income Dummy had, it was against the law. Stark would bet his life on that. Not a smart bet, he thought.

Moving toward the glass door of Eric's, he continued to ponder the problem, but it was not something he really wanted to know. A hustler might discuss candidly the most depraved of sexual practices, but he did not discuss means of livelihood or question others. It was like an unwritten law or something. They lived in the same zone of the underworld, but had nothing in common. They met like this, by chance, at night in the hangouts, exchanged sign language words, but did not communicate. No one did. They were strangers. There was more rapport – even in conflict – between himself and Dorie Williams, than between him and Dummy. Stark shook his head at the strangeness of the world and pushed through the doors. He paused, gazed around the bright chromium and glass cleanliness of the coffee shop, and at the losers and would-be winners who inhabited it.

Dummy was alone at a rear booth stuffing his mouth with an egg-topped concoction of pancakes, the whole mess drenched in syrup. Stark exchanged waves with some of the night people and, almost against his will, made his way to Dummy's booth. He slid in across from the mute and they went through the blindingly fast finger movements to say hello, punctuated by the ritual of winks and grimaces. Dummy's penetrating blue eyes noted Stark's heroin-pinpointed pupils and gestured silently. Stark shrugged, and after ordering coffee made the motion of dialing a telephone; then moved toward a booth at the rear. Lately Dummy made him nervous. He couldn't talk, but his eyes chilled you. They sometimes spoke volumes. He got the sense that Dummy was watching him all the time, warning him. Had he seen him get in the car with the cop?

He closed the phone booth door, dropped in a coin, and, as he dialed, grinned with anticipation. It was three-thirty a.m.

The receiver buzzed half a dozen times before a drowsy, middle-aged female voice answered: "Crowley residence."

"Let me speak to Crowley."

"He just went to sleep," the woman said, uncertainty evident. "Is it important?"

"Yes, ma'am. Life and death."

"Well... I guess I can wake him up. But he's got to be in court tomorrow, so don't keep him."

"I won't, Miss – Miss…"

"Mrs. Crowley," she said sternly. Stark covered his mouth to stifle the chuckle, and then laughed aloud as the other receiver banged hard on a table.

A few minutes later the angry voice of Patrick Crowley came on: "Who's this?"

"Ernie Stark."

"It better be good, to call me this time of night." Crowley's tone wavered between irritation and excitement.

"Pat, I tried to get to the Man for you, but I can't."

"Don't call me Pat, and you'd better… Is that all the hell you woke me up for? Get your ass down to the station in the morning. I'm tired of your fucking bullshit."

"Look, lieutenant, I can get you Momo right away. Ain't that enough?"

"Hell no. You're a worse menace than he is."

The indignation was not fake, and Stark's grin faded. He paused and glanced nervously around, seeing Dummy looking back through the glass doors at him. He wondered what he was thinking. If he knew, it would be a quick knife in the gut or a blast of gunfire from the darkness.

"Is that all you've got?" Crowley demanded again.

"No. I wanted to tell you that Momo's gotten some new junk. Real high grade stuff. His supplier must be getting it straight from outside the country. It's the best shit I ever had, but Momo's not giving up any information. I tried like hell to get it."

"You'd better get it. Now more than ever."

"What if I can't?"

"It's like selling cards. You only get paid for success. If it was up to me, I'd rather have you in San Quentin than anyone I know. You're just a small rat I can use to get a bigger rat. If I can't use you, I'll lose you – quick. You're running out of time."

"Look, man, somehow I'll get what you want. It might take a while but I'll get it. Just don't lean on me. If I can't get it from Momo, I'll work on the broad he's hooked up with."

"It don't make no difference to me. I get my paycheck whether you go to jail or not. If you don't get him, some-one else will. Stool pigeons like you are a dime a dozen."

Stark accepted the contempt silently. Crowley hung up on him. He had a sudden uneasy tightness in his stomach. As he stepped from the booth, he noticed Dummy glanc-ing at him. The mute was writing something on a napkin. He walked back to the table, wondering if, somehow, Dummy knew what the call was about. Dummy handed over the paper. Stark read: "Watch yourself. The cops are on to you."

Relieved, Stark was moving the napkin toward his pocket, before the ridiculousness struck home. It came simultaneous with the mute's almost inhuman chortled laughter. Stark grinned, and playfully threw the crumpled paper at Dummy's chest. "Very funny," Stark signed, but the world was not funny. He ate a hamburger and drank coffee, watching Dummy drive away. By the time he finished, his confident mood had returned, though he did not know why. The fog was even thicker outside. He was in deep and trying to find a way to get out.

In the morning, after less than five hours' sleep, he came awake half-sick. The queasy nausea of withdrawal was beginning in his stomach, and there was the strange aching in his joints – a unique agony he was beginning to experience every day. His habit was growing. He padded barefoot from the bed, wearing only shorts, and fished his stash and outfit from their hideout, drilled into the bottom of the closet door. He fixed before taking a bath, then shaved and smoked the day's first cigarette. While the glow was still on, he drank three cups of hot coffee. Without looking, he knew there was only a hundred and five dollars in his wallet, not much for a guy with his habit. He had to make a quick score, nothing elaborate. He put on a working uniform: clean khaki pants, heavy shoes, and a fur-collared leather jacket over a white T-shirt. On the con, he needed to look like a working man.

Before eleven a.m. he was well north of Oceanview on the Coast Highway, driving through the beach towns that stretched down in a long line from Los Angeles. At a liquor store he bought two-fifths of good Kentucky bourbon, selecting a brand with a unique bottle shape.

South of Long Beach, he parked at a highway cocktail lounge, then carefully crushed down the paper bag so the bottle necks were exposed. Bag beneath his arm, he went inside. The dim lounge was open for early business. The balding, freckled bartender was lazily wiping Bon Ami from the long mirror behind the bar. An elderly, wizened Chinaman was wet-mopping beneath the green vinyl-upholstered booths.

Three customers sat at the far end of the bar. They all seemed to have red eyes and each sipped a Bloody Mary. Two were middle-aged businessmen in rumpled suits. They needed shaves. The third was a tousled, bleached blonde. It was obvious to Stark that she was for hire. He wondered if they'd had a three way motel orgy. They looked like they'd been up all night, and the worse for it.

The trio didn't matter. Only the bartender, and, perhaps, the owner counted. He placed the bag with the bottles of bourbon on the counter and waited the few seconds for the bartender to come over. The man smiled professionally. Stark waited.

"What'll it be?"

"Draft beer... small glass."

"We've only got bottles."

"How much does the cheapest cost?"

The question wrinkled the bartender's face. Partially hidden but still apparent was the inherent disapproval of tightwads and paupers.

"Fifty cents," the bartender said. His eyes wandered to the paper bag. He saw the bottles and was familiar with the brand from the neck shape. Curiosity crossed his face. Stark caught it. Neither spoke, and the man went for the beer.

When he returned, Stark was ready. Fumbling in his pocket, he pinched out a quarter and carefully slid it along the bar.

"Shore wish ah could be drinkin' what ah got in the bag." He twanged the words with a southern drawl and smacked his lips at the end.

"Ain't it yours?"

"Sorta... Leastways after I pay a friend three dollars for 'em. But ah don't get paid 'til next week. Hot damn, it's hell to be a workin' stiff." Stark's eyes were saucer round and bland with simplicity.

"Three dollars!" the bartender said. "That's half the wholesale price."

"Shore is – but ah gotta sell it. Need the money."

"Have you got a buyer yet?"

"Yeah. A guy up in Long Beach. Sold him ten bottles last week."

"Long Beach is twenty miles. You can sell it right here. I'll give you three fifty apiece of them."

Stark deliberated lengthily. "Ah dunno. Ah'm sorta obligated... but it sure is a long drive to pick up three dollars. Ain't really worth the gas. But ah gotta see if he wants more, maybe a whole lot. My friend needs some money... wife's divorcin' him an' he had an accident." Stark continued to ramble, debating aloud the pros and cons of the situation.

"How much more booze can you get?" the bartender interrupted, ignoring the people at the rear who were vying for his attention.

"Hell fire, ah dunno," he said laconically, guzzling a swig of beer and wiping his mouth with the back of his hand.

"Ah guess a whole goddamn warehouse – Scotch, bourbon, brandy, whatever… He ain't never got more'n ten or twelve bottles before, but that ain't cause he can't. He ain't needed no money 'fore now."

The bartender hungrily accepted the information, trying to puzzle the possibilities of the situation.

"Hey, bartender!" the blonde called. "How about a little service?"

"Don't go away," the bartender said to him. "Soon as I take care of these people we'll talk about it." He moved away to fill the orders of the woman and the two men.

Stark had no intention of leaving. He looked at himself in the dim reflection of the mirror and winked. This was going good, better than he expected. First cast of the line and he had a solid bite. The hook was sunk deep. Now to play it along and reel the fish in. The whole thing might be pulled off in two quick meetings, rather than the usual prolonged build up. And he needed dough – fast.

Stark waited until the bartender was at the cash register, then the con man slipped from the stool, picked up the bag, and started leisurely toward the door.

"Hey, mister," the bartender called, coming quickly down beside him. "What's the hurry? I thought we had some business to talk about. Have a seat and a beer on me."

Stark's eyes were again round and naive as he slid back onto a stool.

"Are ya serious? Ah can't be foolin'. I gotta help my buddy."

"I'm serious... maybe about buying the whole lot of it. But give me some details, some facts."

"Well, here's how it is... my name's George Splivens. What's yours?" Stark stuck his hand out before beginning the story...

5

Two hours later Stark was back in Oceanview, cursing in frustration when he discovered that his usual con partner was in Las Vegas. Not that the man was a friend. He was only another predator, wolfish and ruthless, having worked bunco so long that he thought everyone in the world was a potential sucker. For this game, Stark required someone to help finish the score. It was going faster than he expected. The sucker was ready to be clipped immediately, almost begging to surrender his money.

Stark checked his watch. It was after one in the afternoon. Unless he found another partner in a half-hour, he would have to postpone the sting at least a day, and he didn't want to do that. The blood scent of the kill was in his nostrils. Too often suckers cooled off.

He wheeled the station wagon to the Panama Club. In the squalid lair he hoped to find Momo, hoped he was capable of playing the role and willing to do it for a third of the take. It might also be a door open with Momo.

Stark swept to the door and peered inside. It was like any cheap nightclub in daylight, depressing as a hangover. The only occupant was a tired whore draped across the bar. Stark let the door swing shut. Momo might still be in his apartment with Dorie. He couldn't blame him.

Before driving off, Stark glanced down the street. What he saw froze him. Crowley was double-parked on the far side of the boulevard. The detective beckoned him with a meaty paw.

"Christ," muttered Stark to himself, "in broad daylight… the fool." He checked the entire street to see if any local characters were nearby. None could be seen, but someone might be watching, peeking out a window. Stark hated the risk of talking to a cop openly. He shook his head negatively and waved Crowley off. The bulldog face reddened, but the policeman nodded. He pointed down the block, indicating that Stark should meet him some distance away. Stark nodded, and the Ford slid into motion.

He didn't wait to see where the car stopped. The panic had disappeared in an instant. Even as he nodded assent, he had decided to ignore the summons. He ducked back into the vacant club, skirted between the tables, and went out through the kitchen to the alley. Crowley would be pissed, but he'd think of something. The cop would go for a good story. He'd think of one. Right now he needed to find Momo and make some money.

His car was left parked at the curb in front. He could pick it up later. A yellow cab was hailed. Out of habit, Stark got out of the car a block away from his destination. This distance he covered in a swift walk, and when he hit the stairs he broke into a climbing run. He was breathing heavily as he tapped on the door – tapped instead of knocked. In the paranoid dope world a pounded summons was usually the cops. The voice of Dorie Williams came muffled through the wood:

"Who's there?"

"Ernie Stark."

"Momo's not here. He went out."

"Shit," he muttered. "When's he coming back? I've gotta see him."

Dorie misinterpreted the urgency of the situation. "You'll have to come back. I can't sell you anything. He doesn't want me dealing."

"I don't want to geeze. I want Momo. When do you expect him?"

There was a hesitancy beyond the door. Stark could imagine her, face puzzled, perhaps nibbling at a fingernail while her green eyes were clouded with indecision.

"I gotta know," Stark pressed. "I need him for something."

"He should be back in twenty or thirty minutes."

"Let me in. I'll wait for him."

Again she hesitated, but not very long. The lock clicked open, the nightlatch clattered free, and the door swung inward. Stark stepped through, and the girl instantly fastened the locks and braced a chair beneath the doorknob.

Stark stopped in the center of the dreary room and watched her security measures, noting the way her movements caused full thighs and rounded buttocks to press tight against her white Capri pants. These clothes were a better come on for her sexy body than the preceding night's partial nakedness. She turned quizzically toward him.

"You're a cautious creature, baby," he said with sarcasm.

"It's better to be safe than in jail."

"Oh, I'm sure the cops'll get in if they want to. Don't worry about that. I've seen cops crash through more than one door."

"Maybe they will... but it will slow them down enough that I can flush everything down the toilet."

"Good luck. Me, I guess I play it more risky, to the brink of disaster. It makes the game more fun."

"Not me. Besides, Momo gets frantic if I'm not careful."

"You don't have to apologize for being scared of cops – or Momo, either."

"I'm not," she snapped, flushing. "Goddamn you, why must you needle me?"

"Maybe for the same reason it gets to you so quick. Because you're pretty fast with the needle yourself," he tossed off with laconic flippancy and punctuated it with a knowing leer. The double entendre was intended.

"So I like junk. So do you. Big deal."

"Yeah, but I'd rather pay for it in cash."

Dorie's face deepened in color, confusing Stark. He had intended it as a jibe, and her response surprised him. She should not have been embarrassed by his mentioning her relationship with Momo. Slowly, it dawned on him that he had unearthed a truth. He smiled.

She looked at him as if she knew what he was waiting for.

For half a minute they stared at each other, each waiting for the other to make a move. He could see the hint of brassiere pressing its tips against the sheer white of her thin blouse. She stood with her long legs mannishly apart, and as the coloring of her cheeks receded, she threw her head back in defiance. Slowly she put her hands behind her back, the move forcing her full breasts out even more.

"Let's get down to it," she whispered as slowly she began to unbutton her blouse from the rear. When it was free she slipped it off.

She stood for his inspection, breathing in slowly and deeply. Her waist was tiny, her hips wide, and the pants stretched down along every curve of her body. She began to unfasten them, to wiggle and tug them down over her hips. Staring at him, mocking him. Turning him on.

Stark hadn't moved. "We haven't got time for this," he said bluntly.

Dorie froze. She straightened, confusion etching her face.

"Put your clothes back on," he said coolly. "There's not enough time. We'll get around to it, later, when I want you."

It took a few seconds for the truth to sink in. Then, with an angry, sweeping motion, she scooped up the fallen blouse and glared at Stark.

"You bastard," she said. "You cold bastard. You led me on…" She choked back the irate words and tugged up the Capris, but fumbled in fastening them, the impeding blouse in her hand. "So what makes you so superior? You're nothing but a cheap hustler. You're so used to cheap whores, you wouldn't know a good thing when you saw it."

Though his body ached with desire, this was not the time or the place. He enjoyed seeing her anger. It made him feel superior to her. In charge.

"Hell hath no fury," he jibed.

Dorie spun away from him, slipping into the blouse. She stalked to a dusty window overlooking the street and reached back to button herself. Stark could see she was having difficulty. He came up quietly behind her.

"Let me," he said. "I'll do it for you."

She did not answer but her hands dropped in a silent acceptance. As he fumbled with the buttons, Stark touched his lips softly to her ear. She didn't move to accept or reject his touch. She ignored him.

"Don't be mad, pretty," he whispered.

"You're a fucking junkie."

"No worse than you. We can't right now, because your lover will be back."

"He's not a lover. He's good to me."

"C'mon, baby, you don't have to lie. He may be good, but he's still a trick."

"No, he's not. I'm no whore."

"Tell me you love him. Or are you just fucking him? Five minutes after I met you, you said you'd go away with me if he was busted."

"If he was busted, I'd have to go someplace. Not home. My father's a minister. Besides, Momo's been kind to me."

Stark's brow wrinkled. This defense of Momo was completely unexpected. Maybe she did care for the fat Hawaiian. He had no time to discuss it. As he glanced out the window, Dummy's Corvette came to the curb, and from it alighted the object of their conversation. Momo disappeared beneath them, entering the building. The sports car pulled away with a roar.

"Speak of the devil," he said, releasing Dorie as casually as he had touched her.

6

Stark was seated on a chair tilted against a wall, his legs stretched out, when Dorie Williams opened the door.

"He said he had business with you," she explained, taking in Momo's instantly angry glance. "He said it wasn't about junk, and it was important."

Looking at Stark, Momo jerked his head, asking a question without speaking.

"If you wanna make some money real easy and real fast without any risk, I've got a helluva proposition for you."

Momo grunted with pig-like ill humor. Stark realized the response was not to his words, which he'd scarcely heard. This was instead, the reaction of an ugly man insecure with a pretty girl and suspicious of finding another man, a possible threat, inside his home.

"You don't seem very enthusiastic," he said.

"I'm not. You're a con artist. A good one. Too good. What's this going to cost me?"

Stark puckered his lips and shook his head in disbelief. He was careful not to look at Dorie, who hovered inconspicuously near the bathroom door.

"I told you this is found money," Stark said. "I need help on a cinch score. My regular partner is out of town, and I thought I'd throw it your way. I also want to show you how good I am with business. You'd make five big ones, for a couple hours' work."

"Why do you want to do anything for me?" Momo asked, still peering suspiciously, but now his curiosity piqued, the money having been mentioned.

"You can't think anyone would want to be your friend, could trust you, so let's just say I want to keep on the good side of my connection."

Momo sneered, but he could not help sniffing at what Stark said.

"Momo, I wouldn't trust this guy. He's a hustler," said Dorie.

"Ignore the broad. What does she know about business? This is soft and smooth. Now I've got some work clothes down in the car. Let me lay it out and see what you think…"

Twenty minutes later, Stark leaned against the glass wall of a telephone booth and dialed the number of the cocktail lounge on the Coast Highway. Momo stood in the booth's doorway. Both men were on edge.

"Christy's Lounge," the bartender said, "Al speaking."

"Hey, Al… This here's George Splivens, the fella who was in this mornin'."

"Yeah –" excitedly, "What's happening?"

"He didn't wanna. Ah talked and talked for ya. He was scared 'bout his job an' the cops an' all. Ah tole him ya'll was an ol' friend of mine…"

"What happened?" Al interrupted. "Is it all right?"

"Ah was just tellin' ya. He didn't wanna but ah talked him inta it. Can ya get down to Oceanview right now with the money?" There was a pause.

"How soon?"

"Forty-five minutes?"

"That's pretty quick. I've got to get somebody to watch the joint. The owner doesn't know about this deal." Stark could visualize Al's eagerness. He winked at Momo. It was obvious the bartender planned to charge the owner a standard wholesale price for the booze and thereby reap the profit in a quick turnover. It was the oldest profit system, everyone making money except the last guy in line.

"It's gotta be quick. Hell, ah hadda talk like an ol' medicine man to my buddy, an' he might wanna back out, if he thinks about it too long."

"Yeah, okay. It's a deal. I want fifteen hundred dollars' worth. Where do I meet you?"

"Have ya got a truck?"

"I can borrow a panel job from the television shop next

door. I already talked to the guy."

"Then drive on down to Oceanview... Know where Johnson's Liquor Warehouse is?"

"No."

"On Beale Street. Jus' offen the main drag. One seventeen south. Ya park 'cross the street an' we'll be waitin'. Bring the money."

"Okay. I'll be there in half an hour. Goodbye."

"'Bye now."

With a flourish, he dropped the receiver on the hook and playfully slapped Momo on the shoulder. "Let's have a quick drink and I'll write the dialogue for you. The sucker'll be there in thirty minutes. You have to change into work clothes."

At the appointed time, Stark loitered on the sidewalk near where Al had to park. The large brick warehouse and offices of Johnson's were across the street. Momo was there, hidden in the shadows of a sealed-up doorway, unseen from where Stark stood or Al would park.

Stark jammed his hands down in his khaki pants and propped one foot against a wall. He appeared to any onlooker like one of the poor working stiffs common to industrial neighborhoods. A figure that attracted no second glance. But his eyes were not dull or lifeless like those men. His were shifting, carefully examining every delivery truck that sped past, knowing that many carried goods highly saleable on the hot market, where he had many fences. It was another of his hustles to pick out one of these trucks, especially those carrying garments to retail stores, and follow it on its route. Even if it took all day, eventually the driver would make a mistake and park in a bad spot during a stop. In the few minutes it took the man to go inside, Stark could remove a thousand dollars' worth of suits or dresses. It was swift and easy, requiring only a jimmy bar, timing, and boldness. Now he looked at the passing vehicles to see something worth examining for another day. He would remember the company name of a likely prospect. He had a very good memory for possible jobs. He'd always had a good memory, even in school. He could have gone to college, but crime was more exciting. The hustle got his adrenaline going. It beat studying for exams.

A few minutes later, a blue panel truck with the name of a television repair shop pulled to the curb. Al could be seen through the windshield. Stark pushed away from the wall and came swiftly to the passenger side. He opened the door and slipped in.

"Hey there, ol' hoss," he said, grinning toothily.

Al was fidgeting nervously, gripping the wheel tightly. "Is everything all right?" he asked tensely.

"Shore nuff is. Don't be worryin'. This here's easy as takin' candy from a baby."

"You can say that. You're not breaking the law. I'm taking the risk. Me and your friend. Where is he?"

"Hell, I ain't takin' no risk, but I ain't makin' much money either. All ah done, ah done for my buddy. Ahm hardly makin' change in this deal. You don't seem to 'preciate that."

Al looked sheepish. "You're right, man. I'm sorry. I'm just nervous. But where is he?"

"Should be 'long any minute."

They waited and almost as if on cue, Momo appeared from the doorway. He was wearing a uniform of polished blue cotton such as those used by service station attendants and delivery men. On the breast of the shirt was embroidered the legend: JOHNSON'S WHOLESALE LIQUORS. The uniform gleamed in the afternoon sunlight. He paused for a lull in traffic and then came over. He'd bought the outfit for a hundred bucks from a former employee. It was the best investment he'd ever made.

"Is that him?" Al asked.

"Sure is. By gawd he's a good boy. Give ya the shirt offen his back." Al watched Momo approach. Stark leaned back in the corner and studied Al's florid face in profile. The confidence man was looking for some flicker of suspicion. There was none.

Momo came around the front of the truck to the rider's side where Stark sat. He didn't open the door but stepped on the running board and peered inside.

"I can't stay. One of the girls might see me from the office window. Is this the guy, Spliv?"

"Sure is."

Momo eyed Al with feigned suspicion. "I'm not so sure."

"He's all right. Al's my buddy," Stark said. He almost winced, though, as he looked at Momo. The drug peddler appeared sinister as a Mexican hood.

"I guess it's okay then," Momo said. He looked at Al. "Did George tell you what to do?"

"More or less."

"I'm foreman on the loading dock in the back. I fill the orders. When you drive in back, park near the west end and I'll take care of it from there. You'll be getting twenty cases of top of the line bourbon. Give the money to George. I don't want to carry it back there. He'll tell you just what to do. I can't stay." Before Al could protest, Momo nodded quick goodbyes and ducked around the back of the truck. Stark could see the bartender's confusion and moved in quickly so the man could not call Momo back.

"It ain't good somebody should see him talkin' to ya. They can see out the window an' you're goin' in thar right now. They might think it was kinda funny."

"Yeah, I guess you're right," Al said, grudgingly bringing his eyes away from the departing figure. "I didn't get much out of him, though. Is he Mex?"

"He's dark, but he's originally from Hawaii. He just wanted to see ya – make sure ya was okay. Ah'll tell ya what to do."

"You ever done this before, either of you?"

"Naw, we ain't habituals. But we done talked it over a whole lot. Ain't hardly nothin' can go wrong." Stark reached over and clasped Al's shoulder to give him reassurance. "Say, man, ya been frettin' like an ol' bull fulla Spanish fly without a cow. It's all right. He runs things back there."

Al chuckled, suddenly relaxing. "Maybe I am worrying too much. Now just what do I do?"

"Ya go in theat door right over thar, an' ya fill out an order for two or three cases of whiskey. Ya pay for it an' they give ya some papers. Ya take the papers 'roun the back... so the people see ya hand them to Willie. He tells 'em what to put in the truck."

"I take the truck around the back?"

"Yep. Unless ya wanna carry it home."

"No, I don't want to do that." Al was now in a good humor. He shook his head. "If that's all there is to it, it's pretty easy. Where are you going to be?"

"Wall, ah can't go in back with ya. Some of them swampers know ah'm a friend of Willie's. Ah'll wait here 'til you come outta the office, then I'll get the money and leave."

Al nodded. "When do I start?"

"Go right now. They close in about thirty minutes. An' Willie's probably nervous as a cat on a hot tin roof right now."

Al quickly activated himself. Patting his right hand pocket (Stark saw the move and knew the money was there), he exited the truck and went across into the building. He watched him go; then, lighting a cigarette, he got out and went to stand beside the panel truck. He wanted to be on the sidewalk when Al returned.

The bartender's face was beaming when he came back. In his hand was the red, yellow and white triplicate order form. He came around to where Stark stood.

"How'd it go?"

"Like silk. Like you said. Man, we can do it regularly."

"Ah don't know if my buddy wants to. This is only 'cause he needs the money... fact, ya better give it to me now. I don't want you takin' off with the booze and our dough." Stark extended his hand casually, but his veiled eyes noted every move that might show the man's thoughts or reservations. There was a brief flicker of uncertainty.

"It ain't for me. My friend said to get it," Stark said quickly.

Al laughed. He was trying to copy the off-handed manner. He brought out a roll of fifty dollar bills and surrendered them. "Want to count it?"

"Naw. Hell fire, we gotta trust each other, an' there ain't time. Now you hustle 'round there an' get your stuff."

"Damn right we have to trust each other. If we can't, who can we trust?" Al grinned, thinking his comment humorous. Stark wondered if the man would grin if he knew how funny the statement really was.

He smiled in return, and winked. "Ah like you. Damned if ah don't. Better get goin'. He'll be worried. Ya saw how he is. Ah'll give ya a call tomorrow. Maybe we can do this again, six months."

"Great. Great. Thanks for everything." The bartender extended his hand and Ernie Stark shook it firmly. Al went around to enter the truck.

The moment the blue vehicle was in motion, Stark

started toward the corner and quickly went around it to get a taxi. Momo came from the doorway and scurried to catch up. When they were together they began to laugh spontaneously, envisioning the expression of horror on the bartender's face when the amount of the triplicate order was loaded on the truck — that, and no more.

7

Minutes later Ernie Stark and Momo Mendoza were speeding down the highway in the back seat of a taxi, faces lighted with the exhilarated satisfaction of predators who have made their kill and gorged themselves on red meat. Both were high on the successful con.

The taxi driver was a gnome-faced runt with ears like a bat's wings. A procurer of servicemen for the prostitutes of the Panama Club, he was a close-mouthed underworld fringe character, so Stark and Momo were not afraid to talk freely.

"That's the softest money I ever saw," Momo said, shaking his head in wonder.

Stark's eyelids fluttered and the smile of a Cheshire cat played across his thin lips. He nodded with fatuous complacency. "Yeah, real sweet bunco... but —" he shrugged and let the thought trail off.

"But what?" Momo asked. "There's nothing wrong, is there?" the quick suspicion of the paranoid junkie in his voice.

"No, everything's lovely. We won't even have any heat, nine chances out of ten."

"Won't the sucker call the fuzz?"

"Not usually. He can't say how the swindle went down or the Board will jerk the bar's license... padlock the joint and put him out of business."

"That wasn't the owner."

"The owner is responsible for his agent's actions. And the feds wouldn't like avoidance of the tax on liquor sales, either."

"Is that right?"

"Yeah. And the one thing that drives bar owners out of their minds is worrying about losing their license. They pay a shyster a grand to represent them at a hearing for something as simple as a juvenile buying cigarettes out of a machine... No, they won't go to the fuzz. They just lick their wounds and mark it down as a loss. A few might try to find you and get their money or fuck you up, but it's like they're trying to find a needle in a haystack."

Momo shook his head in slow wonder. "Man, you should be making a million dollars with a gimmick like that. It's the slickest game I ever saw."

"Yeah, I've made some money," he said in a depressed manner. "And when I do, nowadays you usually wind up with it." Yet he noticed the respect, even awe, that was in Momo's voice. It was a sharp change from his previous attitude to him. Momo had made the switch without seeming to remember the arrogance of yesterday, or even this morning. It made Stark even more contemptuous of his dealer. This new relationship might be used to good advantage, for himself and perhaps Crowley.

"It's sweet," Stark agreed, "but I've burned it out. About fifteen bars have bit in the last eighteen months. The word gets around. I tried one spot a couple of weeks ago and the owner set me up to get my arms broken. A couple of goons were waiting in a parking lot. I cut one and ran. Seems I trimmed the guy's brother somewhere down the line." Stark shook his head. "Yeah, it's just about burned out. All good things come to an end, I guess. You're the one with the best hustle. There's never a depression in your business, and you can make big money if you can get enough shit. There are more customers than you can handle."

"I can get the product," Momo announced proudly, "but Oceanview ain't got but a few junkies. I just got enough business to keep up my habit. Ain't no big action here."

"If I had your connection I'd do more than that. I'd be crappin' in tall cotton... not living in a bust-out pad making nickels and dimes. That broad could be wearing mink, and you could be driving a Caddy."

Momo rubbed a hand hard across his face, as he might do upon just wakening. He probed a nostril with a fingernail and snorted. Stark could not tell if these gestures had any meaning, or if the man's mind had wandered. Stark decided to be more specific.

"In a month we could be selling five times what you're moving. With less risk. We'd have an organization with other people in front. We should get together and work out something real good for both of us. Besides, I figured that this new shit was coming to you from a bud back in Hawaii. I haven't figured out how you're getting it into the country."

Momo laughed. "This shit is coming from no further than La Jolla. I don't have any friends left in the islands."

For the first time Momo saw the possibilities. His surly face registered the kernel of an idea. His lips pursed, and his brow drew down. Stark watched him as a hawk might, high above a rabbit. The Hawaiian sucked a substance from his teeth, probed for it with a forefinger, and shook his head.

"Man," he said, "if you'd made me a partnership proposition last week I'd have laughed. I used to think you were just a lot of words, pure bullshit. After today, I give you a whole lot of credit. Let me think about us working together. It's just an idea. Don't rush me."

"We'll make a sackful of money. I'll find us new customers all over the place."

"But I don't think I can cut you into the connection. He won't meet anybody. He's weird. The product has to come through me – only."

"Oh, yeah," Stark said slowly. He paused, then accused: "What's wrong? You don't trust me? Think I'm a snitch or I'll ace you out of the connection?"

"No, man. I got to protect myself. As long as I supply the product in our partnership, you won't have the opportunity to ace me out. Besides, the Man is very nervous." He spread his hands wide, a gestured plea for understanding. "He won't go for it, and he'll freeze me out if I try. He doesn't know about hustlers. He's a square-john businessman trying to make a killing on the side. He's scared of his shadow. He doesn't even know I use. You don't need to meet him. I can make the arrangements for what we need."

Momo spoke with such plaintive sincerity that Stark knew he couldn't press further at this point without losing ground.

"You're right," he said. "I don't have to know him. We can make money anyway."

"Sure. We'll try and see what happens." Momo hesitated, then looked Stark coldly in the eye. "One thing, though, I'm not sharing that broad."

"Ah, man," Stark said, poking Momo reassuringly on the arm. "I know she's your property."

The object of Momo's admonishment was not at the apartment. According to a scribbled note, she had gone out to a movie. Momo accepted the information with his characteristic grunt. He was in a good mood and chattered with glee about the easy five hundred dollars he'd just made. He listened attentively to Stark's brief sketch of the plan. They would enlist peddlers in the nearby small communities. Each had at least one base, a cocktail lounge or a pool hall, and a handful of junkie customers. The junkies presently had to travel fifty or more miles to Los Angeles to make purchases. Stark would set up one dealer in each area to work on consignment initially, and a runner to make the deliveries.

"But we'll work it out later," Stark said as they finished fixing. He also pocketed two free grams for later. "There's a lot of details, but that's the basic idea. I've already got an idea for the runner, somebody who can't run his mouth. Dummy."

Momo burst into wild laughter.

"What's so funny?" Stark asked.

"Dummy!" gasped Momo, "as a runner!"

"What's so funny about that?" Stark asked irritably.

"Nothing, except he's my runner. And you don't want to cross him. Believe me."

Stark rode another taxi downtown. He sat in a drug-induced snooze and let a cigarette burn down to finger-searing shortness, before flipping it from the window. He mulled on the puzzle of Dummy and the Man, wondering how he could track the guy to his quarry. Yet, try as he might, Stark could not associate Dummy with any businessman in Oceanview, nor anywhere else. Stark reached through his memory for any clue, but finally had to shake his head and put it off until he had more facts. The connection was still anonymous. Now, however, the bits of knowledge were filling into place. He'd find him. And maybe turn him in to Crowley. And then again, maybe not. His idea for a new dope network was beginning to seem attractive. Maybe it could work. Maybe Crowley would have to get another boy.

8

It was easy enough to find Dorie Williams. The beach community had only three movie theaters, and only one of these showed weekday matinees. There were only a handful of patrons. She was in an aisle seat, halfway down.

Stark halted, while still unnoticed, beside her. A malicious grin crossed his face. He leaned down and dropped a hand firmly on her shoulder.

"We want to talk to you at the station, Miss Williams," he said coldly.

Dorie jerked at the touch and words. A reflexive gasp issued from her. Stark knew the panic she felt. He chuckled as she turned to see what she assumed was a cop.

"Oh, you asshole," she said. "You fucking creep. I thought you were a cop."

"Funny, huh?" he said, sliding past her legs and plopping into the next seat. On the screen John Wayne was mauling the villain.

"Good movie?" he asked.

"It was awful, until you got here. Now it's worse."

"Then let's get out of here."

"You're crazy. How'd you find me?"

"I got your note."

"I left that for Momo."

"You put his name on it, but I knew it was for me."

"Did you steal it?"

"No."

"You're awfully sure of yourself..." Her voice rose sharply and stood out against a sudden lull of sound on the screen. Someone nearby made an irate "shhh" sound.

"Come on," Stark whispered, leaning close to breathe in the sweet scent of her perfume, and putting a hand gently on her arm. "We didn't have time to talk before... We've got time now. I want to continue our conversation. Don't you?"

Dorie wavered, looked into his face in the flickering dimness; then, with a sigh of resignation, gathered her purse. He hungrily watched the swish of her wide hips as he followed her up the aisle.

It was dusk when they came out of the theater. Oceanview's main drag was crowded with traffic hurrying from work, with square Johns and Janes trying to finish shopping and get home. Cars choked the streets in a honking tangle, crowds jostled in and out of the stores. A breeze was rising. In the deepening twilight the neon signs were throwing off their first glow, a halo-like aura that had not yet grabbed enough darkness to be brilliant. Dorie waited on the sidewalk. The breeze whipped her skirt against her legs.

"Where should we go?" she asked. Her voice was thick and tense.

"He won't worry about you for a couple of hours."

She nodded slowly and dropped her eyes.

"Yes. I have about two hours."

They hesitated, waiting for thoughts to jell. The pedestrians broke around them and hurried on. The street's traffic struggled forward.

"We can have a drink… or we can go to my place."

"Whatever you want." She looked at him. He could not tell whether it was with surrender or hate. Stark took her arm and they started toward a cab stand.

In the taxi there was silence for the first few blocks as he wondered why he was taking her to his pad. Then they were beyond the downtown section and the automobile picked up speed.

"Is it very far?" Dorie asked.

"About ten minutes' drive." Stark looked at her in profile against the backdrop of a red sun sinking into the sea. Hers was not a hardened face. There was something childish and undefiled – or perhaps only half defiled. It was not purity, really; neither was it evil. He did not know what it was, but it was fascinating.

"I don't know why I'm doing this," Dorie said, speaking suddenly. "I don't like you. You're no good. Momo's a crude animal, but you're like a snake with shiny scales."

She spoke so quietly that Stark could not become angry. Instead, he felt dirty. He needed to lighten her up. He needed to lessen her loathing. He thought that humor might do it. "Maybe it's like Bess and Crown – you know, in 'Porgy and Bess' – she couldn't stay away from the evil Crown, even though she loved Porgy. When Crown called, she had to go." He spoke in a semi-singing voice, jocularly.

She responded with seriousness, "You might be closer to the truth than you think."

They both fell silent. Only the whoosh of spinning tires and the click of the taxi's meter broke the silence. Stark looked at her closely, the length of her. This was the first time he'd seen her fully clothed, wearing a dress. Her garb and makeup were not those of a whore shacking up with a penny ante dope pusher. She was dressed in modish style, but not garishly. There was nothing visible to suggest that she would come so easily to his bed. And it was even stranger that this paradoxical girl, ready to give her body to him, would put up a defense of Momo Mendoza.

"What's with you?" Stark asked. "I can't figure you out."

"What do you want to know?"

He was stopped. She confused him more every minute. He cleared his mind of the jumble of feelings and tried for coherence.

"I'm interested in you. There's something..." He

stopped again, angry at himself for the sudden loss of words. "I mean, what do you want? What's your kick? What're you looking for?" he asked.

"Everything's my kick. Everything there is."

"And Momo. What do you see in him? He's poor, even if he supports your habit. He's ugly, and he's got the manners of a pig."

"The doctors at the hospital said I want to degrade myself, to punish myself. He's as good a whip to beat myself as any. Maybe that's what attracts me to you, too." Her voice was modulated to half-humorous truth. Her green eyes held mocking laughter, and her lips became a bemused smile.

"Ask a crazy question, get a crazy answer."

"They said that, too... that I was crazy. Let's not talk about it. Too much talking about yourself leads to spiritual hypochondria. When there's time, we might get to know each other, what we are. Not here, not now."

Stark nodded. She was good with words, just as he was.

When they entered the apartment, darkness was only a few minutes away. The drapes of the large, beach-view window were drawn apart, showcasing a sea that was blood red in the last edge of sun, blood deepening to black with coagulation.

Dorie went to the window and stared out at the sunset. The room itself was dark and her figure stood out in silhouette against the crimson sky.

"You look like a beautiful painting," he said from the shadows.

She turned to him and her features were not visible, only the auburn tresses which glowed at their fringe. She laughed, and it seemed out of context in the dimness. "Don't change character on me," she said. "Don't get sweet. It doesn't suit you. Nice view."

Stark flicked on the lights. They were soft but brought the mood back from the melancholic to the sensual. He put some jazz on his record player. Dorie strolled around the living room examining the comfortable furnishings. She scanned two Renoir prints. The place was neat, orderly.

"You've got good taste," she said. "Better than I expected. You give off a whole different vibe."

"We're even. I expected you in whorish clothes and painted face."

Their eyes came together in silent laughter – then they were locked in spontaneous wordless communication.

"Where's the bedroom?" she asked huskily.

Stark's mouth was suddenly dry, and the blood began to pulse at his temples. "Do you want a fix first?"

"Afterward," she said.

She followed him to the bedroom door. He held it open, and as she brushed past he could smell her perfume and feel the warmth of her. Wordlessly, she began to turn back the pale blue bedspread and blankets. The smooth white sheets gleamed, another surprise. Dorie stood beside the bed, facing him, the fingers of her right hand brushing gently and thoughtlessly along the sheets. She was waiting for him, head tilted back, mouth parted in a challenging provocation. She dared and challenged him in the same glance.

"Take your clothes off," he demanded coolly. "Do it slow, the way you started to back there. I want to watch."

She smiled at the command in a way that was a mere drawing back of the lips, and yet it was more sensual than anything she might have said. With slow, flowing movements she began to undress, the smile still on her mouth, her eyes never releasing their hold on him. Her earrings were unpinned and dropped on the nightstand. Her dress was unbuttoned at the top and slipped down over round, milky shoulders. She let it fall to the carpet and stepped clear with the poise of a stripteaser. She stood there in panties, bra, high heels, and stockings. The white full thighs above the sheer nylon made Stark lick his lips. She twisted her torso into a partial profile as she unfastened the bra. Her high breasts, pale and full, wiggled as they came free. She took them in her hands and cupped the bottoms, holding them up for inspection, arching her back slightly to exaggerate the curve. With wide, bland eyes she turned to see his reaction.

Stark's breath hissed in and out of clenched teeth. He swallowed dry and couldn't speak. He was mesmerized by her.

Dorie sat on the edge of the bed and extended one leg in the air. "Come take my stockings off," she said. "I know you want to."

He moved forward and kneeled before her, hands damp as he wrapped fingers around the warm firmness of a raised thigh, and rolled the nylon down. The heady scent of perfume and femaleness intoxicated. She had beautiful long legs, and when the stockings were on the floor, he kissed her knees, then higher.

"No, don't," she said. "Take your clothes off first. I want to feel your body next to mine." She held his head away.

Stark slowly stripped as she had. He was letting the tension build. He gently lay down next to her. She rolled on her back and pulled his face down to her breast; she was whimpering with desire. He stayed cool, in control, until they were joined. She urged him on. "Fuck me. Fuck me hard."

And he did.

Afterward, they showered quickly, rinsing the sweat from themselves. Stark slipped into doeskin slacks, kicking the discarded work clothes into a corner. He carried a white shirt with button down collar and a cashmere sweater into the living room where Dorie was fluffing her hair and applying makeup. Dropping the garments on the sofa, he placed a paper of junk and an outfit on the coffee table.

"How long before Momo starts worrying?" Stark asked.

Dorie took the lipstick tube from her mouth. "I should be back by eight, I guess."

"That's still almost an hour. It takes about fifteen minutes. We've got time to fix and call a cab."

"Where's your car?"

"Parked at the club. I left it under duress, sort of. I'll

ride with you and pick it up." He gestured toward the equipment on the table. "How much do you want?"

"None. I don't want him to get suspicious."

"I need to geeze. After that little score today he took me in as a partner. We're in business together."

"As a partner." She shook her head. "He should know that his new partner just fucked his girl."

Stark paused in the heroin cooking. He glared at her, his good humor suddenly gone.

"What's your story, bitch? I get tired of you always putting the know on me like I'm some kind of dirt. You've always got a snide remark. It shouldn't bother you what I do to other people. Just worry about yourself… what I do to you."

"I worry about that least of all," she said in a quiet way that blunted his anger, "because I don't really care what happens to me."

Stark concentrated on preparing the fix, but he was trying to find precisely how he felt toward this girl. In the first place, it was hard to define, because he did not understand the contradictions of her personality. Moment to moment she changed: from prissy schoolgirl to slut to warm, tender woman. She was intelligent and could turn on the charm. Perhaps it was the many facets of her that held his fascination. An attraction he found hard to deny. In the idiom of his world, maybe he was weak for her. Certainly she was becoming important to him. Even letting her know where he lived was a first. It was not characteristic of him to sit around thinking about someone, except as an object for use or misuse. He realized suddenly that he wanted her for longer than the stolen moment. It was the first time he had ever needed a woman other than to fuck. The realization was stunning. He shook his head and forced himself to think about the delicate matter of getting high.

Dorie had finished grooming herself and was standing beside him.

"I'm sorry, baby," she said, "I shouldn't bug you. You're a wild lover. There's just something that makes me do it. Maybe it's something in me... I don't want you to be good to me. I don't want you to change."

"How's that? What could be changed?"

"The hardness in you, I guess. That might be changed."

Stark stared at her, wondering whether to reply with honesty, deceit, or laughter. He decided on the latter. "It's a good thing that you're not looking for a nice guy. That ain't me. I look after number one. Me."

Dorie shook her head. "You've got a hard shell, but you're weak underneath. You think you're cool. You're not. You think you're smart. You're not."

"Fuck it. Let's go to hell together."

She shook her head again, this time emphatically. Stark did not press the issue, though he did not forget it either. He stood up, holding the full syringe in his fingers. "Here's to hell anyway."

9

Stark entered the Panama Club as he had last departed it – from the alley at the rear into the kitchen. This was not out of fear of Crowley. It was merely that the club was closer than Momo's apartment, so he exited first. It would not have been prudent to have some hood see him arrive in a taxi with Momo's woman.

He glided through the odors of cooking and slipped into the main room. He was met with the hubbub of laughter, the tinkle of glasses, blaring music, color and movement, and floating layers of cigarette smoke. He knew many of the occupants, but spoke to none. He crossed the room, planning to get the car. He wanted to drive and mull over the problems of Momo, Crowley, Dorie, Dummy, and the unknown big connection. It was sure as hell complicated. He wanted the girl, but she wouldn't leave the skib. Even if she would, Stark could not afford to incur Momo's anger right now. Not that Momo mattered, but without him, Pat Crowley's hammer would fall. There would be no Dorie, or anything else except prison for several years.

There was the beginning of a thought about somehow crossing Momo not only with the girl, but with the big connection as well. If only there wasn't the ever-looming hulk of a police lieutenant. If only he could set Momo up for the fall, ease the pressure, and leave a clear field with Dorie and the Man. He could then be a major pusher. This would be the way to come out ahead. How to go about it was the dilemma. If he only knew Momo's hidie-hole.

Stark was preoccupied with these swirling ideas as he covered the short distance down the sidewalk to the old station wagon. He stepped around the rear and took out his keys.

From the darkness across the street issued the beam of a spotlight, splashing him. The cops. He whirled, blinded by the glare, heard the click of car doors opening, and his first horrified thought was of the heroin in his pocket. He dug it out as feet pounded towards him. Uniformed shadows with drawn guns loomed up as he stuffed the small bindle in his mouth.

"Swallow, you bastard, and I'll blow your head off!" a voice boomed.

Stark threw his hands in the air. "What's this?" he cried, and though terrified, he swallowed what was in his mouth.

No murderous gunshot sounded, but a fist came from the darkness and crunched into his jaw, sending his body crashing into the car and red lights through his brain. He drew his arms over his head and crouched down.

"Goddamn, what the hell is this? What's going on?"

"You stinking junkie," the voice said in rage. "I know what you did. I should shoot you. Run, dammit, run so I can shoot."

"Ma ain't raised no damn fool," Stark quipped, still cowering beneath his hands.

A calmer voice sounded. "Take it easy. Let's cuff him and take him in."

Rough hands spun him, fastened his wrists in crushing steel bracelets behind his back, frisked him, and then jerked him away from the car by the manacles. He was shoved, stumbling toward the police car. Once out of the spotlight glare he could see he was in the clutches of young harness bulls. Obviously they had staked out the station wagon.

He was shoved headfirst into the rear of the prowl car and face down on the musty floorboard. The door slammed shut and a foot pressed down into the nape of his neck. His legs were doubled back against the closed door. It was a cramped, filthy position and an uncomfortable ride. Yet his attitude was not of anxiety or even really discomfort. Shock had not worn off enough for these things to be evident. If he felt anything, it was an undirected, numbed disgust at the whole mess.

At the station the cops hustled him up the back stairs. At the directions of a uniformed sergeant, they locked him in a holding cell, a windowless, bedless room, air-conditioned to a chill. A bright fluorescent light was set into a screened recess in the ceiling. It gleamed down on a metal bench bolted to a wall and a dull aluminum-cast toilet bowl along another wall. They were the extent of the furnishings.

The handcuffs were removed and he was left alone. He did not need to check his Spartan surroundings. He had been here before. Nor did he need to know why he had been picked up. There had been no questioning, which meant the pickup had been on Crowley's orders. The detective was still angry at being brushed off in the afternoon.

"He must be real mad," Stark muttered, patting his pockets and finding the battered pack of Luckies in his shirt. He sat on the bench and smoked, rubbed his sore wrists, and waited for Crowley.

Three cigarettes later Crowley had not arrived. Stark leaned against the door and peered out through the tiny glass window. After ten minutes of waiting, he saw a detective come down the corridor. He banged on the door and the man came over to the crack.

"Where's Lieutenant Crowley?" Stark asked, pressing his lips to the corner of the door. "I want to see him."

"He went home fifteen minutes ago," the detective said and departed.

Stark cursed under his breath and went back to the bench. "I'll be a sick sonofabitch in the morning. And he's a dirty sonofabitch for doing this."

The first hours were not uncomfortable or filled with dread. Shit did not allow pain or worry, but created a sense of being removed from the drama. He knew precisely the reality of the situation, but as if it was happening to someone else, a character in a motion picture.

Because of his disassociation he was able to hold the facts and turn them different ways. He lay on the bench, head propped on his rolled up jacket. He smoked incessantly until the cigarettes were gone, pitching the short butts unheeded on the floor, and later re-lighting the larger of those for a few more puffs. Meanwhile he reflected on how to handle the situation. There was no doubt that this was punishment and a scare by Crowley. After a night of torment and some conversation, he would be released. But by the same token, this arrest was a clear indication that his time was running short. Crowley's patience was strained and he would not accept further stories or delays.

Yet Stark could not formulate a definite plan. He hoped, as usual, that he could play the scene by instinct and make the right decisions in the moment of crisis. Still, even a general outline eluded him. He knew he wanted too many things, and could not make all of them mesh together. It would be simple if he could trade Momo and his connection. But he couldn't bring himself to do that. Not that he cared about the still unknown connection, or his own underworld morality. It was only that by using him, his new partner, he could become more successful. A year of being a big dealer and he could buy a chain of cigarette machines and a small nightclub. Even keep Dorie. He lay there, smoked, and shook his head.

After midnight the first pains of withdrawal commenced; the tremors of pain increased minute by minute to become, after a few hours, an agony blotting out virtually every other thing. Logical thoughts were swept away. He writhed and kicked and puked and cursed the sickness.

By morning he was so weak that he could only stumble to his feet when Crowley unlocked the cell. His usual sleek appearance was rumpled and foul. Drops of spattering vomit had dried on his shoes and the cuffs of his trousers. His matted hair was wild and his clothes were creased with deep wrinkles.

He stumbled against the door frame as he marched past the well-fed, morning-chipper detective, who smirked at the wrecked apparition.

"You look just fine this morning," Pat Crowley said genially.

"Stick it in your ass," Stark said with as much fire as he could raise. He staggered along the sterile corridor and the red-faced man lumbered behind. From experience Stark knew where to go – a soundproofed interrogation room. Despite the agony, his brain functioned, though not with the clarity of the previous evening.

"Sit on down, chum," Crowley said, closing the door

and waving him toward a chair behind a bare table.

Stark flopped down, shivering with a sudden chill. He did not see the flash of a grin on Pat Crowley's face. The detective slid a pack of cigarettes across the table. "Have a smoke."

"They'd taste like something from a sewage plant."

"You don't feel so good, huh?"

"You know damn well how I feel," Stark snapped, managing a splutter of anger.

"Serves you right, punk," Crowley capped back with more sarcasm than anger. He spun a chair around across the table and squatted on it, his forearms crossed on the back. Stark was sweating and yawning and twisting. Crowley watched him as if studying something new, though he had seen countless sick junkies in his career. "It must be real good," he said, "for anyone to put up with the agony when it's gone... and then go back to it again every chance there is."

Stark didn't answer. In his sickness he wished only to get over the matter at hand.

"Well, Stark, you're smart enough to know this is just a slap on the wrist for ducking out on me yesterday."

"I couldn't... something was happening right then," Stark interrupted.

Pat Crowley waved him quiet. "I don't want to hear it. You didn't come, so I sent for you. Now you're sick and I don't really give a damn... 'cause you're just a piece of garbage to me. You already know what I think about you. But this time you're getting another chance. You're still useful to me. But when I say 'shit' after this, I want you to squat and start grunting real hard. Understand?"

Stark's head was slumped forward, but every word was heard, and he nodded. He was too sick even to hate the arrogant bastard.

Crowley paused in his one-sided conversation long enough to fire up a cigarette. He exhaled in a stream. "Now what've you got for me? Anything?"

Stark shook his head.

Crowley glared. "To hell with it. I'm gonna throw the key away on you." He pushed himself from the chair. "Let's go down to the booking desk."

Stark forced down a gasp of nausea. "Wait… a second. I'm not feeling good. I think I got something."

"It better be good."

"I'm sick… can't talk," Stark croaked. "Gimme a fix so I can tell you."

Crowley raised himself to full height and sneered. "You're joking. Spit out something I like and you can go back to your cesspool and fix yourself."

Stark flinched, steeled himself, trying to control his trembling body. "The big connection is in La Jolla. I thought his shit was coming in from Hawaii, but it's a local operator."

Crowley's blue eyes twinkled with interest. "That's not good enough for your bail. Give me some more. Who's the Man? Where does Momo hide the stuff?"

Stark shook his head. "I don't know."

Crowley appeared disgusted. "You're not making much

progress. Maybe I should let Dummy know that you're trying to rat out Momo."

"Momo's taking me in as a partner. I'll find out who his connection is. Momo's going to introduce me to him… but it might take a couple of days. The Man is very cautious. Dammit, you're driving me to my knees. Ease the pressure." Stark suddenly went into a quaking, teeth-chattering spasm. Though the worst of it passed in a few seconds, he still vibrated visibly. "Got a plan," he gasped. "Gimme something so I can talk… can't like this."

Crowley nonchalantly dropped the consumed cigarette to the floor and ground it beneath his heel, mulling slowly on the information. "We don't have medicine for sick junkies. I'll let you get your own. You go and call me this afternoon or you'll kick your habit in a cell." Crowley's eyes bulged with emphasis.

Stark nodded once, jerkily. "Where's my car?"

"Still on the street. I didn't plan to keep you so it wasn't towed in. A prowl car can drop you off."

"Just get me a cab."

"Suit yourself. Wait here while I clear you downstairs."

Crowley walked out, leaving the door ajar. Stark moved only once – to lean sideways and vomit a few bilious leavings from a wretched stomach. He waited in a silent stupor and could not think of anything beyond his next fix. It felt like he was dying. He had told himself that he wasn't a real junkie. Just liked a taste once in a while. The night in the cell proved otherwise. He'd have to cut back.

10

It was only luck that kept Stark from having several wrecks as he drove like a madman from the Panama Club to Momo's. He ran a stop light without seeing it. A two-ton truck screeched and swerved to avoid collision and was banged by a following automobile. Stark drove on heedlessly, weaving through traffic, blasting the horn frequently, and cursing the slower cars.

At Momo's he forgot his normal caution and parked directly in front of the doorway. He scrambled out and ran up the stairs, not slowing his pace as his stomach retched and dry-heaved.

At the door he pounded, then leaned in weakness

against the frame, panting as if having a heart attack. Nobody responded. Stark waited less than a minute, then squatted on his haunches and peered into the keyhole. It was blocked by the key inside. He pounded harder.

"Momo! Dorie! Open up. I'm sick! I know you're in there."

"Who is it?" Momo asked. From the voice Stark knew he was just inside; and the voice was shrill and taut.

"Ernie Stark."

There was another pause. "Are you alone?" Momo asked.

"No. Your mother's with me... For Christ's sake, open up. I'm sick out here... sick!"

"Wait a minute."

Stark cursed silently. From within came the muffled sound of movement. Seconds ticked off that seemed hours. He raised a hand to knock again just as the key was turned. Momo's face appeared behind the nightchain, eyes wide as he peered beyond Stark to see the hallway. He allowed the nightlatch to clatter free and Stark weaved inside, bending slightly forward with stomach cramps.

"I need to geeze," he said.

Momo fastened the door but did not move away from it or speak. Stark caught the silence and was puzzled. He looked around for Dorie. She wasn't in the room, but in the corner behind the door stood Dummy, his clothes gleaming with Italian-silk elegance, a gigantic .45 dangling in his hand. The mute's face wore its usual inscrutability.

"What's this?" Stark asked, panic mixing with pain. "Why the heater?"

Momo came away from the door.

"We didn't know who it was. You scared us with that racket... sounded like a platoon of cops." He motioned Dummy to come forward and then faced the closed bathroom door. "Dorie, it's okay, come on out."

Dorie Williams appeared, carrying a lidless shoebox. Over its rim, he could see the contents: several plastic-wrapped packages of shit. Obviously she had been sent into the bathroom to flush it down the toilet if the pounded summons proved to be the police. Had Dummy just made a delivery?

"Cook a jolt for me," he begged, going to the bed and he flopped down. He was too ill to notice that nobody moved. Momo and Dummy stood together, watching him; Dorie faded to the background.

"Where you been?" Momo asked.

Stark raised his head, saw the hardened faces, and propped himself on an elbow. "I've been in the police station. You know damn well where I've been."

"You weren't booked," Momo said with suspicion. "Dummy saw you get pinched, and I had a bondsman call the jail."

Stark scanned each of their cold faces and Dorie's frightened eyes. He sneered at the gun in Dummy's hand. "What's wrong with you, Momo?"

"I want to know how you got out so quick."

"I finked on your mother. She's going to Alcatraz...

Man, don't be stupid. You're acting like a sucker... you and that no speaking fool. I got out because they didn't have any case. It was just a roust. I swallowed the last bindle I had before they rousted me. They had no proof, but grabbed me anyway."

"You didn't tell them about me. About us, did you?"

"Man, I'll tell you about it when I'm fixed. I feel too goddamn bad to talk." He trembled suddenly as if to demonstrate.

Momo blinked, thrown off-stride by the surly barrage. He managed to hold his ground, however. "I want to hear something right now."

"They thought if I went cold turkey overnight, I would talk. I didn't, so they let me go. They ain't here, are they?"

Momo nodded, satisfied. He touched the mute's arm and signaled to put the gun away. It disappeared into a shoulder holster. Dummy motioned Momo to follow him to a corner of the room where he took out a small tablet and scribbled a message. The Hawaiian read it and nodded yes. Dummy gestured that he was leaving, stared hard at Stark, ignored the girl, and departed.

"If my stomach wasn't empty," Stark said, "I'd puke over your bed. What're you gonna do?"

"Man, I'm sorry. Dorie, get some stuff out. We've gotta give my partner some medicine."

Minutes later, Dorie and Stark were alone in the bathroom. She cooked the fix. There was no conversation until after he jerked the needle from his body. The nausea disappeared so quickly that it seemed never to have existed.

He stretched himself, wrinkled his nose at his own odor, and eyed Dorie. She had scarcely looked at him since he entered the apartment.

"What's up, baby?" he whispered. "Why the cold shoulder? I thought it was you and me…"

"I didn't like to see you sick and weak. It made me feel bad. I don't like to see anyone in pain."

"The world is pain, baby. The whole world gets hurt. It's a jungle with lions, foxes, and snakes. I'm all of them when the times call for it. Look at how I handle those two fools in there. I turn them on and off like a light." He spoke with such contempt that it brought a flush of anger to her face.

"Always the con artist, but Dummy didn't buy your story. Didn't you notice?" she said. "And to think I felt bad for you." She spun away. Swiftly he stepped forward and grabbed her arm, restraining her while he leaned close to whisper.

"Listen to me. Get it straight. I'm a loner. My old man was a junkie. I've been in this life since I can remember. You're a newcomer, and you've still got your church upbringing with you. You don't really know what's with this fast life, and you've never met anyone like me, but I've never met anyone like you, either. I will hurt you." He added quietly, "But, I wish I could trust you. I don't know why." He was flushing, unable to say more.

Dorie's face mirrored her own confusion. The pang of longing in his words – so unexpected – embarrassed her. She could not answer, did not want to answer, and instead moved back into the other room. Stark, back in control of his feelings, followed.

Momo had a large sheet of glass on the bed. Piled on its surface was an ounce of heroin. He was deftly pressing empty capsules into the pile, filling them. A box of orange toy balloons was beside him. Each time ten capsules were filled, they were popped into a balloon. This was tied into a knotted top. If only Crowley could see this shit.

"Did you get fixed good?" he asked.

"Yeah. Real good. It even wiped out the aches where those cops punched me."

Momo nodded terse satisfaction and gestured toward the materials on the bed. "Help me cap up some stuff. I wanna get finished quick."

"You're in a hurry?"

"Yeah. I've gotta drive down to Malibu."

"That's pretty high class."

"I've got a good customer there."

"Pretty high class territory for a dope fiend. And out of your stomping ground."

Momo dabbed the capsules. "C'mon and help."

Stark pulled up a chair and began to fill capsules. "In fact," he added as an afterthought. "Malibu is so high class the guy shouldn't be called a dope fiend. He's an addict, poor devil." Stark grinned at his own humor.

"He pays double the regular price," Momo explained. "That's why I make the run."

"That's cool. Maybe you should cut some of this good shit. He might not notice."

Dorie went around the bed and started putting the filled capsules in the balloons.

"You made me feel bad," he said, "throwing guns on me, like you doubt our partnership."

"That's Dummy. He was so frantic it bugged me for a minute. He kept shaking his head and making those funny sounds. He doesn't like you. Doesn't trust you. Says I shouldn't either. I'd watch myself with him, if I were you. What'd you ever do to him?"

Stark's eyes went suddenly narrow and veiled. His hand paused in midair. "Is that right? I've known him a long time. We were in the same prison together. Everyone was scared of him in the pen. He had a bad rep. I tried to be friendly back then. It didn't take."

Momo shrugged.

"I don't know. It's something. I think he's nuts. He shivved a guy in prison," Stark added.

"Did he really do that?" Dorie asked.

"Sure. How else was he gonna get a rep in the slammer? Cons leave the nutcases alone."

"Forget it," Momo said. "Try to stay out of his way."

"I ought to kill him for thinking I'd turn in my partner," Stark mumbled with pointed viciousness.

"Man, be cool. It's nothing. You're okay with me. Otherwise you wouldn't be my partner. He's just a runner."

Stark nodded in a way that accepted the advice grudgingly, though the threat of murder had only been for effect.

"Forget Dummy and find us some dealers. The faster

we get moving, the faster we make money."

"I'll drive to Santa Ana this afternoon while you're gone."

When they had fifteen balloons of capsules, Momo stopped them, gathered everything else together, and carefully replaced it in the shoebox.

"It's time for me to go." He spoke so that Stark knew he must also leave.

"Give me a couple grams," he said. "One to fix and one for a sample."

Momo tossed over three full balloons. He got his coat and told Dorie not to leave and to keep the door locked. The statement about the door was for Stark's benefit.

The men went out together and separated on the sidewalk. They planned to meet at the Panama Club in the evening.

He drove a few blocks and pulled into a service station. While the attendant was filling the tank, Stark went to the telephone booth. He stared at the black instrument for half a minute, then with resolve dropped in a coin and dialed the police station. He asked for Pat Crowley and was connected.

"I've been waiting for this call," Crowley snapped, before he could do more than announce himself. "Get your ass down here."

"I'll be there in ten minutes after you listen to me. But if I do, I'm not going to be any good to you. I've got burning heat. That pinch last night damn near got my guts blown out."

"What happened?" Crowley asked, suspiciously.

"Dummy might be wise. He rammed a gun in my stomach 'cause somebody got suspicious about my night in the station without charges. I talked my way out of it, but let's not press our luck. Dummy is on my case. He must suspect something. He is definitely the Man's security."

"Interesting. Watch yourself. You're no good to me dead."

"Yeah, thanks. I also know what will happen. You can believe me or not. Like I said, I'll come in if you force me. But you'll be trying to get me killed if you do."

Crowley's lips smacked over the receiver. "Hmm… Okay, I'll go for it. I don't want your murder on my conscience."

"Thanks, friend… Another thing. The scene slowed me down. I don't want to press Momo for the connection for a little while. He doesn't suspect me – unless there's a seed in his small brain. He thinks I'm trying to freeze him out with his broad. He'd think differently about the connection if I pressed too hard."

"You mean you've failed. Is that it?"

"No. I mean I've got to go slow."

"How slow?"

"A few days. Max a week. How should I know? Until I get his confidence up."

"What've I got to lose?" Crowley thought aloud. "I can always put an APB out on you. And I've already gone for so many of your stories that one more won't hurt. Just keep in touch so I don't get paranoid and need to send for you again. This time you'll get the long rest cure."

Stark came out of the booth, weak with relief. He paused to light a cigarette and considered the situation. He'd had no plans on leaving the apartment beyond the phone call, and the sudden lightening of pressure left him vacant. He had been like a man spun toward the beach on a giant ocean wave, fighting for a single breath of air and not concerned beyond that point. Suddenly, Crowley had tossed him a life preserver. The wave would eventually sweep back for him, but meanwhile he could breathe and plan and act.

Drawing hard on the cigarette, Stark was almost giddy. Relieved now, he realized how great the strain had been. He had won a victory, had toughed it out, rode the punches, and played all ends successfully against the middle. Arrogance rippled through him. Now Dummy might be his only problem.

"You're a fat fool, copper," he muttered. He flipped the cigarette defiantly against the tire of a passing automobile. The butt cast a small explosion of orange sparks. He swaggered away toward the station wagon. He decided to do what he had promised Momo: drive forty miles to Santa Ana to see someone about pushing junk. It was what his partner wanted. And the plan of organization would go on even if something happened to the partner. Setting up a good network might lead to a lot of possibilities. Instead of delivering the Man to the copper, he'd get rid of his partner when the time was right, by letting

Crowley know where he kept his goods.

"That poor Hawaiian," he said without pity, wishing he had someone who could appreciate his intrigue.

11

The station wagon left a billowy wake of dust in the afternoon sun; Stark drove slowly down the unpaved road, checking the faded numbers on the dwellings against that in his address book. The dead end street – leading to orange groves – was on Santa Ana's outskirts. Though the houses he passed were not really old, their cheap construction and lazy residents had caused rapid deterioration. Nor were there sidewalks or lights, and the street's original coating of gravel had been worn away by time, leaving only the dust to rise.

Near the end of the block, Stark found the address. The white stucco bungalow, set far back, was more unkempt than most of its neighbours. The paint was streaked with reddish stains. The screen door was ripped and sagging. What had originally been a large front lawn was so over-grown with tall weeds that it looked like a vacant lot. A derelict automobile, entrails ripped out, stood forgotten on blocks at the curb. In the driveway a roadster hotrod with upflung hood was being worked on by a bare-chested kid in greasy Levi's. He turned to stare without expression at the beat-up station wagon.

Stark slid across the front seat to the window, expect-ing some greeting. There was none, so he opened the door and stepped out. The skinny, freckled youth moved a few feet forward.

"What you want, man?" the youth asked; his manner and voice were challenging.

He grinned, trying to ease the suspicion. "I'm looking for your brother. Anyway, I think he's your brother. You look like him. Alfie."

"Oh, yeah. Who are you?"

"Not a parole officer or the fuzz."

Before the boy could respond, the screen door squeaked open and out popped the head of a hard-faced slattern wearing a red bandanna as a hair scarf. "Who's that, Clyde?" she called.

"A guy lookin' for Alfie, Ma."

"A friend of his," Stark added.

"If you're a copper," she yelled, "he ain't here, and he ain't gonna be here."

"Ya don't know where ah could find him, do ya,

ma'am?" Stark called, hoping a southern drawl would ease the hostility. "Do I look like the heat?"

"He oughta be in hell… but he's likely in some honky tonk with some junkies… like you. An' ya better get outta here or I'll call the law."

"Ah sure ain't no junkie, but I'll get to gettin'."

"Ya no damn good, whatever ya are."

He was already turning to leave. Clyde stepped closer and spoke so his mother could not see or hear. "You'd better split before she calls the cops. Alfie's probably at the Pit Stop."

"What's that?"

"A roadhouse two miles on the highway. If you see him, tell him I'll be there tonight."

"I'll tell him. Thanks."

He went three miles outside town, in the direction of Los Angeles and found the roadhouse. Only four cars were in the front parking lot of the nondescript building that had been designed as something other than a night spot. It was ugly, gray, and low, and the original broad windows had been painted over. On the highway shoulder was a blue neon sign. A larger sign rose from the roof. Both announced: PIT STOP. COCKTAILS. DANCING. A banner dangled down the front of the building to announce that Arnold Hunter's combo played there three nights a week.

Stark knew the brand of entertainment to be found there after dark. Places like these sprouted on the highways outside cities and catered to a trade that was fast and loud and undiscerning.

He got out and pushed through the heavy doors. The interior was dim and cool. The tables had been roped off, but the long bar was open, though there were only three customers — two young women in dresses too sleek for daytime in the hot weather and this rural setting and a slender young man in a filmy white shirt so soft as to be almost feminine. His sandy hair was clipped collegiate short and he was sipping a Tom Collins.

Stark came up beside him. "Alfie."

The young man turned. His face was clean cut, tanned, and liberally freckled. His green eyes were clear and bright. He was in his early twenties. He grinned, exposing even, pearly teeth. "Ernie Stark, you punk! Where's the ten dollars you borrowed?"

He laughed. "Man, the statute of limitations ran out on that debt."

They shook hands. He took the adjacent stool and ordered a Tom Collins to match Alfie's. The bartender moved away to make it.

"Forget the dime," the younger man said. "I learned more than that from you in jail. I didn't think I'd ever see you again."

Stark tossed a shoulder. "You never know in the underworld."

"What brings you around here?"

"I was looking for you."

Alfie's clean face wrinkled. "How'd you find me?"

"Your kid brother. I went by your pad. He gave me the address. By the way, he said to tell you he'll be in."

"He wants some weed. You're lucky he was there. My ma wouldn't tell you."

"She wanted to call the heat."

Alfie laughed and shook his head, then sobered. "Anyway, what brings you? Are you on the lam?"

"No. I got a proposition. You look like you're doing all right."

"You taught me some tricks. I've got a little broad hustling out of here, and I'm the night bartender. It isn't a million, but I haven't got any heat and that T-bird out there is mine... mine and the Bank of America."

"Are you using?"

Alfie shook his drink around and stared into it. "A little. I ain't hooked. Why? You got some?"

"If you want a fix... Where can we get gear?"

"In the toilet back there. I've got a 'fit."

The bartender brought his drink and when Stark reached to pay, Alfie waved him away. He said to the bartender: "Tab me for it."

"Thanks, sport," Stark said.

"Ain't nothing. Anyway —" Alfie grinned, "I give you a drink and you give me a fix. I'm ahead."

Stark took a swallow from the sweet cocktail. "Pretty good. It'd taste better after some junk. Let's go geeze."

"You must be hooked," Alfie said, moving off the stool. They went down the bar toward the rear.

"How many junkies in Santa Ana?" Stark asked.

"Nine or ten... hooked. Fifteen or twenty more who use stuff once in a while."

"You know 'em?"

"Most, I guess." He opened the door to the men's room and bolted it when they were inside. From beneath the sink he brought out an outfit wrapped in a handkerchief. They stopped talking until the eyedropper was squeezed empty into their veins. Alfie dabbed soap on the tip of his forefinger and carefully massaged the red dot on the puncture on his arm.

"This is fucking great shit," he said huskily, then faced Stark with glazed eyes.

"So what's the deal?"

"Let's go back outside."

Alfie hid the outfit in the same niche and the men went back to the gloomy main room. The girls had departed, and the bartender glared disapprovingly at the men. He guessed what they had done. But it was none of his business, so he kept away.

The iced liquid tasted especially good to his dry mouth. Alfie was waiting. The men put their heads together and in soft tones he related the plan to Alfie. The younger man's All-American face was chiseled hard as he listened; his green eyes blazed with the naked intensity of the hunter as he followed what was said. Yet, he did not glow with enthusiasm; his interest seemed remote. Stark sensed the reserved attitude and halted his pitch.

"What's wrong, man? Don't you want to get involved? If you don't, maybe there's someone else here who wants to make some money and keep up a habit. It's a good deal.

The supply will be steady, and there'll be a runner making the drops."

Alfie shook his head. "It ain't that. I'd go for it myself only I don't think you can move enough stuff to make it worthwhile."

"Why not?" There's ten dope fiends buying steady and that's two or three hundred a day gross. Those others who chippy will get hooked if the supply is steady. You know how that goes."

"The supply is steady already."

"Somebody else dealing?"

Alfie nodded. "Not somebody from around here. One of those high rolling Mexican dope peddlers had the same idea as you. He's got a guy making a run every day. Not only in Santa Ana but all the other little towns around here. I heard they're bringing the shit in carloads."

"Sonofabitch," Stark cursed.

"The shit ain't as good as yours, but most of the real customers are Mexicans and they'd buy from another Mexican first. There's not enough customers for two connections."

Stark was deflated. While laying out his game, he had sold himself. His own words had added to his imagination. Now there was a major problem. A competitor. Silently, he glared into space.

"Aw, fuck it," he said. He sucked violently on his cigarette, exhaled the smoke in a tight stream as an expression of anger, and then mashed out the butt, sizzling, in the leavings of his glass. A scowl darkened his face.

"Fuck this, now I got to worry about goddamn Mexicans," he snapped in frustration.

"I know it's a drag," Alfie said with a shrug. "I'd like to pick up a few hundred a week… And it'd be so soft. There's no heat on heavy narcotics around here at all."

"I wish I could say that about Oceanview." Stark thought of the jowled face of Crowley. He knew that it would not be many days before the cop stormed back down on him with both flat feet. He winced in anticipation. The mood of confidence he had felt while driving to Santa Ana was now dispelled, despite the shot he'd just had. His habit was growing.

"Man," he said. "Here I got the best product, but no way to get it to the market. And I'm surrounded by fucking Mexs. I don't like to snivel, but man oh man, you can't imagine the hassles I've been in."

"If you need some bread, I can let you have fifty. You won't pay it back, but I can afford it."

"No. I don't need money. I need a smile from God, something."

"I ain't got no drag in heaven," Alfie grinned, then sobered, shaking his head. "I don't know what to tell you. I can imagine how you feel, sitting on a gold mine with no way to get it out."

"My partner looks Mexican, but he doesn't speak Spanish. He's Hawaiian. Would they buy from him…" He trailed off, and his thoughts drifted to the situation of Momo and Dorie. Any intense feeling for a woman in his world was a sign of weakness. Dope fiends, thieves, and pimps would chuckle and ridicule. In fact, Stark found it hard to admit his growing attachment for Dorie, even to himself. He resented having her so constantly on his mind. He pushed away the problem and attempted to talk of other interests.

"Have you seen anybody from the felony tank?"

"A couple hoosiers," Alfie said. "That old check writer Martin comes in here on the prowl for young chicks. My old lady ripped him off a couple of times." Alfie gazed at his glass and fingered it, looking to attract the bartender's attention. Then he suddenly brightened. "Hey, remember those two kids in the last cell?"

Stark searched back. "Johnson and Kleger. Yeah, I remember."

"They stopped by here a couple times. They're burning up with heat. They've been heisting everything in the state from Sacramento to San Diego. They shot up a market in Stockton. They're only young punks, but they've got a pocketful of money and shoulder holsters with big pistols. They swaggered around here like they were Dillingers, had two drinks apiece and couldn't stand up. My old lady balled one of them for a hundred pesos."

"They've got a short life expectancy."

"They're making money. Living the good life."

"That's good," Stark said, sneering. "They'll have memories during all the years they'll serve. When they get pinched, if they don't get killed, they can kiss everything off for a dozen years."

Alfie's enthusiasm dulled under Stark's bleak response.

The younger man flagged the bartender and motioned toward the glass.

"Yeah, they're damned fools," he muttered. "They're staying at some dump called the Rendezvous Motel just the other side of Disneyland. They called up and wanted me to score some weed and bring it to them. I passed. Man, I wouldn't get around them and maybe wind up in the middle of a gun battle with the cops. It ain't my style. Those gunsels are crazy."

Stark shook his head. "I know what you mean. The whole game in the underworld today is just to survive and stay low. Scenes of shotguns and heavy capers belong back in the thirties."

The conversation died a natural death, each of them drifting off.

He finished another drink and excused himself. They exchanged telephone numbers, Alfie giving that of an apartment and Stark the Panama Club.

"If you get anything going, get in touch with me," Alfie said. "I want to get enough together to buy a bar of my own and retire."

"At twenty-eight?"

"The best time."

"I may have an angle. Can you set up a meet with the local Mex dealer? I'll call you."

"Give me a couple hours' notice."

Stark got up and gestured goodbye. Alfie sat quiet.

"Don't take a hot shot," he said, smiling. Stark squeezed his bicep in a comradely gesture, winked, and then walked outside to blink in the dazzling yellow ferocity of Southern California sunlight.

The highway was a torrent of vehicles, swift projectiles of cars whipping past relentless trucks. He joined this river, holding the station wagon in the slow lane behind a school bus carting boisterous high school students home.

The Dodgers game was on the radio, and he listened with partial attention while he examined his dilemma. It wasn't anxiety gnawing at him, but rather a plodding anger. He featured himself as a man swordfighting several opponents simultaneously, and unable to take enough time to finish one off.

The idea came with startling suddenness. In an instant, he had the whole plan, and after a more deliberate examination and certain modifications and additions it got even better. It was a move of finesse to checkmate Pat Crowley, use the Mexican network, and pave the way to double crossing Momo. It struck him as being so clever as to be hilarious. He began to laugh. He laughed so hard that he almost didn't see the bus in front of him come to a halt. He stomped the brake and swerved wildly to avoid a collision. The crisis momentarily sobered him, but as the highway opened again, he grinned at the beauty of his plan.

A glance at his wristwatch told him there was still time to reach Los Angeles. He began to watch for the first cut-off to turn around. He was excitedly nervous the whole way.

12

The powerfully built man with slate blue eyes and the flattened nose of an ex-prizefighter sat behind the cluttered desk, listening intently, meanwhile thoughtlessly fingering an unlighted meerschaum pipe. Covering much of the wall behind him was a map of Southern California. He was the state's chief narcotics officer for the region.

Stark's story and proposition spilled out in a driven mumble, accompanied by hand-wringing worry and a fearful demeanor. He was whining and servile, keeping his eyes down – though his mind was razor sharp. When he ran out of words, the man behind the desk held up a hand to restrain him. A silence ensued. The officer reflected, frowning on what he'd been told.

"It's interesting," he said. "It's reasonable, but it's strange as hell. You're coming here to set somebody up because Lieutenant Crowley – I know him – made a deal you can't keep."

"It's the truth, Mr. Wilson. I can help you but I can't get what he wants. He isn't interested in East L.A. or Santa Ana. It isn't his territory. But it's yours. If I can get out of this mess, I'll straighten up my life."

Wilson snorted. "Don't toss me that crap. All you want is some daylight." Wilson mused again, face wrinkled. Prickles of doubt rose in Stark; he watched for some sign. Finally the man made a decision. "I haven't got anything to lose. You wandered in here on your own. I can't tell Crowley what to do. But I can talk to Pat and he'll go along with me, I'm sure. I've heard about this delivery operation. It's pretty big. Those small towns don't have much of a narcotics squad so it's up to me."

"I want to do this," he said, and he wasn't lying.

"Are you sure you can do it?"

"That's why I came. Haven't I told you the truth?"

Mr. Wilson nodded slowly. "Yeah, I've got to say that. How long before you can set it up?"

"Like I said, I'll do it my way. I'll be able to get the runner tomorrow, but we'll wait a few days until I can get next to his boss. Then I'll arrange something like a big delivery and you can get him on the way."

The state agent slowly filled his pipe with tobacco, his

unblinking eyes never leaving Stark as he did so. He did-n't speak until he had finished lighting the pipe and the smoke curled around his face. He seemed to stare into Stark's soul.

Stark felt naked, nervous. The man frightened him. He wished he hadn't come here, yet he searched for something more, hoping to turn off the penetrating gaze. Then, he remembered something.

"This isn't a narcotics problem," he said, "but there's a couple kids who've been heisting markets... trigger happy punks. They're wanted real bad. Johnson and Kleger..."

"What about them?"

"They're holed up in the Rendezvous Motel, near Disneyland."

Wilson reached for a telephone. His attitude toward Stark was now more relaxed. Stark sighed and looked out the window. It was getting late in the day; the smog filtered sun was just beginning to wane.

It was almost dark when the station wagon slowed its plunge to enter the outskirts of Oceanview. The boulevard lights cast their brilliant, sterile glows, spilled in pools onto the asphalt, flashed across the waxed enamel of hurtling automobiles and made them gleam in varied hues.

He had the car radio on, listening to the soft music and waiting for the baseball scores. The hourly news broadcast mentioned events in the far corners of the globe, and then, closer to home, tersely mentioned that a highway patrol-man and a bandit had been slain in a gun battle at an

Anaheim motel. Dead were Officer William Canton and a twenty-year-old, identified as ex-convict, Donald Kleger. Stark's ears focused. A second bandit had been flushed with tear gas and captured. The officer was survived by a wife and three children.

"Shitheads," Stark muttered, thinking of Kleger and Johnson. "That's what they get for playing Dillinger..." One was dead and the other would go to the gas chamber for the cop – which wasn't really a bad trade. He felt no guilt over what his tip had caused. He wished he could trade a criminal's life for a cop's more often...

A minute later they were forgotten. He was imagining Crowley and the look on his fat face when Wilson told him. It was worth a chuckle. Maybe Crowley would work himself into a heart attack and die. Only that was too much to hope for. As for the Mexicans, they were so dumb they wouldn't know how or why they'd been caught.

Momo's apartment was less than a block off his route, so Stark stopped there. But the tenement dwelling was empty. He drove on to his own apartment to bathe, fix, and change clothes. On the way back to town, he halted at a beachside steakhouse, leisurely consuming a chop, and propositioning the indignant waitress.

It was nine p.m. when he drove slowly past the door of the Panama Club and scanned it to make certain no police cars were at the curb. He pulled around the corner and parked in the shadowed side street.

He pushed into the clamorous room and stepped aside, eyes shifting over the scene. No cops. A flashy pimp was

earnestly lecturing his sulking whore in a manner threatening violence. He watched momentarily, lips curling
back in a leer; probably the bitch had come up short on
some money or had spent too much time with one trick.

A group of marines with loosened blouses and bloodshot eyes were at a table, trying to sing along with the
rhythm and blues number on the gilded jukebox. A tired
barmaid was serving them bottles of beer, while dexter-
ously avoiding their pawing hands.

Through the smoke and noise, he located Momo,
Dorie, and Dummy at a table in a corner. A young man
Stark knew as a local junkie was standing before them,
hands pressed down on the edge of the table talking
intensely to Momo. As Stark moved forward, he could see
that the guy was sweating rivulets and trembling in
spasms.

"…money tomorrow, I swear to God, Momo…"

Momo's face hardened to the plea. Dorie seemed pale
and embarrassed by the whining. Dummy's cold eyes
stared at the agonized face of the begging man. He could
read his lips

"What's up?" Stark asked, coming beside the man and
speaking to Momo.

"This fool wants some shit on credit. He thinks I'm a
fucking bank."

Before answering, he patted Dummy, comradely, on the
shoulder, noting him stiffen at his touch and glare at him.

The junkie turned to Stark, his face twisted into anger
caused by pain. He seethed at the intrusion, though he

knew Stark by sight, if not by name.

Before the man could say anything, Stark jumped in. "So you want some junk on credit… You look pretty sick."

The man hesitated, not knowing what to say. Finally, he nodded. "Why? You got some?"

"Umm hmm. I might give you some credit."

"Man, I'm sick."

Momo opened his mouth to protest, but he waved him silent.

"It'll cost," Stark said. "Carrying charges are business."

"How much?"

"I'll give you a gram for fifty dollars."

"That's almost three times the usual," the man whined.

"Who ever heard of buying on credit? There's two things that's cash and carry in our world: junk and pussy. If you don't like the tariff, cruise on up to L.A. and see if you can get credit."

"I can't drive that far. I'm sick."

"Nobody would cuff you if you could. So you're stuck with my price. What do you want to do?"

The junkie's face shattered into deeper seams of pain. Tears welled up in his eyes. Stark almost sneered as he was already fingering what remained of the capsules in his pocket. He knew, exactly, what the guy was going through.

"When do I have to pay?"

"The next time you come to score. If I'm not here, give the money to Momo. And if you don't have it, better leave town. We'll find you."

The man nodded jerky acceptance, even as Stark was slipping the balloon from his own pocket into the man's sweaty palm. The purchaser spun and rushed out, bouncing off a table without losing stride. In a few minutes the memory of the pain would disappear.

He pulled out a chair, winking at Momo. "You didn't really think I was getting weak, did you?"

"I didn't know. Do you think he'll pay?"

"Sure. He pays or leaves town. You're – we're – the only connection. Anyway, it was only a little over half a gram."

"You're rotten," Dorie said disgustedly. "The guy was in pain. Didn't you just have the same experience? Where's your heart?"

"Shut up," Momo snapped.

"Yeah," Stark said laconically, eyes burning into hers. "Just keep quiet. You're not sick. You don't have to steal or sell your pussy to keep from getting sick. So worry about yourself. You can't carry the world on your shoulders. That's the way it is in this life – cold and rotten. Dog eat dog."

Dorie flushed, and fell silent.

Stark faced Dummy and exchanged greetings in sign language. The mute responded, but his manner was tense. Stark asked what was wrong, and Dummy shrugged him off. Just pointed a finger at him, like he was holding a gun. The response brought a flicker of anxiety, for he remembered the pistol in the mute's hand earlier in the day. For a moment, he had a flash of real fear, but quickly turned to important business with Momo.

"I saw my guy in Santa Ana. I've gotta go back in a few days, but it's gonna be all right. He can move about an ounce a day."

"Shit, that's more than I'm moving right now."

"It ain't nothing. Tomorrow or the next day I'll drive over to San Bernardino and Riverside and see some other people. We're gonna be shittin' in tall cotton."

Momo gleamed. "Yeah, man." He looked to Dorie, sipping her drink, her eyes downcast, still stung by Stark's words.

"You hear that, baby? We're gonna be making big money. I'm getting us out of that crummy pad. You'll have some clothes that'll stop traffic. We might even get you a little sports car. How's that sound?" Stark watched Dorie's face. He could see that her smile was forced and insincere. It wasn't gifts that Dorie needed. Momo didn't notice but rattled on about the big Cadillac he was going to buy himself.

Dummy paid no attention. He was staring across the crowded room at a young Eurasian prostitute in a tight dress split at the knee. She was a newcomer to Oceanview's tenderloin. Stark knew the mute sometimes purchased sex and frequently took it without payment, but only from whores who couldn't go to the police. Long ago, an indignant pimp had challenged these freebies and had been shot dead for his protest. There had been an arrest, but there were no witnesses. Since that time Dummy was accepted as an occupational hazard by the local whores. They preferred to submit and avoid the possible bruises and black eyes for resisting that might put them out of business for a while. In fact, most of them seemed to enjoy Dummy, who had a rep for bizarre sex.

Stark ordered a drink and fished out a cigarette. He had no matches and signaled Dummy for a light. The mute took out a book of matches and flipped them instead on the table. He ignored the obvious slight, lit up, and closed the matchbook. He glanced at the gold lettered advertising on the blue cover. He started, for a moment, trying to disguise his reaction.

Aztec Travel Agency, La Jolla, California.

The Aztec Agency specialized in tours of Old Mexico, said the back of the matchbook. There it was in neat gold script. There it was: the Connection. There was no doubt. Someone at the Aztec Travel Agency was Momo's source of supply. That was where Dummy, the runner, had picked up the matches. Why else would Dummy be in a travel agency? In La Jolla?

Feigning casualness, Stark tossed back the matches, checking to see if anyone had noticed his surprise. Nobody had. He puffed on the cigarette and guzzled the drink, the alcohol mixed with the excitement churning him. The puzzle was almost together, except for a few minor pieces. Later he would formulate a plan to use the information. Now, he had to be cool, though he couldn't help but imagine how Crowley would like to know. Yes, it was a precious bit of knowledge for several reasons. It was another commodity to barter on the information market if things got tight. More important, it was the last obstacle to acing Momo. All he needed was to work a deal with the Man, and he already had a rough idea of how to go about that.

Dorie's voice broke into his gloating reverie. "You look like the cat that ate the canary."

He winked and grinned. "That's how I feel, baby. Things are going good, better than we expected. Hell, we're gonna be in fat city any minute. Think of all the good things your old man will get you."

Dorie's face clouded slightly. Stark saw it, but Momo did not. He was slightly drunk, and affectionately reached over to squeeze Stark's shoulder.

"That's my partner," he said.

Dummy watched; his ice blue eyes gave away nothing, but seemed to see everything. He was like a cobra, wound up and ready to spring. He was cold. Real cold.

A chorus of raucous laughter exploded from the table of marines as one of them leaned too far back in his chair and crashed to the floor. The jukebox dropped another platter to the turntable, and a trumpet sound screamed into the smoke and laughter and tinkling glasses. The Panama Club throbbed with frenzied people and the neon life, trying to escape reality.

13

Stark came awake with the sudden completeness of a wild animal. He had caught an alien sound through the growl of surf and the darkness. Someone was quietly coming up the wooden stairs, outside. He swung silently out of bed and padded to the dresser. From a drawer he took out a loaded .25 automatic, and cocked it. It was small, but still deadly.

Someone was knocking softly at the door, insistent.

The gun was for unexpected callers. Only Dorie knew the address. If it was the police – his thoughts went to his stash. He would throw both the junk and gun out another window to the beach. They couldn't want him for anything so serious that he couldn't make bail.

But it wasn't the police, they didn't knock softly. Instead of going to the door, still in shorts, he moved through the four a.m. darkness to a side window, where he could peer out on an angle to the landing. She stood in the shadows. She knocked again. He stared down into the blackness below, but there was nobody with her. He pushed open the window and she turned at the sound. He could not see her features in the gloom.

"What do you want?"

"Oh, I'm so glad. I almost decided you weren't here."

He grunted, closed the window, and went around to open the door. He still carried the pistol and was naked except for the shorts.

Dorie stepped inside and Stark locked the door, turning his back toward the bedroom without looking at her.

"Why the gun? Is that another pistol in your shorts?" asked Dorie, with a leer.

"What are you doing here? Did you tell anyone you were coming here?"

Dorie followed him to the bedroom, taking off her coat. She cradled it in her arms and stopped just inside the door, leaning against the frame.

Stark pushed the automatic under the mattress and reached for his pants on a chair. The girl's arrival at this hour was a complication he didn't need. Not yet.

"I left him," Dorie said to the question he hadn't yet asked. "I couldn't take it anymore."

"Does he know you came here, came to me?" he interrupted.

"Does it matter if he knows?" Dorie's green eyes stared at his lean face.

Stark fastened the belt and rubbed his unshaven jaw; it was flexed tight with growing anger. "Hell yes, it matters."

"Why?"

"You're jiving! You know damn well why. We're just getting started as partners, and he's got the Man. I need that connection to make big money."

"We could move to Hollywood. I've got a couple grand in the bank."

"We'd shoot that much in our arms if we've got to buy retail. Anyway, you wouldn't make that much hustling in a few months after you were hooked real good and the dough ran out. It shows up bad on a broad." Stark began to pace, shaking his head.

"Does he know where you were going?"

"No."

"That's one good thing."

"I shouldn't have come," she said in a tremulous voice. "I thought you wanted me."

Stark sighed, reached for a cigarette, and fell back on the disarrayed bed. He looked at the girl in the doorway and shook his head. She looked like she belonged on a college campus or in a hick town beauty contest; clean and wholesome, yet sexy as hell.

"Sure, I want you," he said. "But why the hell did you

have to make the move right now? In a few days he won't be able to do anything about you. Why now? I thought you liked him."

"I despised him all along... He was drunk tonight – you saw – and he said he loved me, wanted to get married. Imagine that... the pig. Love and marriage. I know I'm into punishing myself, but I'd rather kill myself."

His face was quizzical. "So he loved you, and he's a pig. You knew that he was a pig all along, and you've been opening your legs to him. Up to now you didn't want to scram. Now 'cause the slob loves you, the party's over. I don't know how to figure you."

Dorie turned her large eyes to the carpet. Before speaking, she sat limply down on the foot of the bed. "Let me have some of that cigarette."

Instead, Stark put a match to another and passed it over. She blew out a cloud of smoke and stared intently into space.

"What's your story? Explain it," he asked, propping on an elbow to watch her.

"I can't love anyone," she said. "And I don't want anyone to love me." Her words were said with a slow matter-of-factness that was more emphatic than any emotion could have been.

Stark opened his mouth to say something smartass, but instead licked his lips and shook his head. He knew that he would only get deeper into confusion, into a realm beyond his understanding.

"That's why I'm here," she went on. "You want to freak

off and use my body. Maybe you want to use my mind. You're too cold to fall in love with anyone. You're a hundred times colder than Momo. He's just a slob, not really evil. You're evil. You just want to use people. You don't love anyone. You can't love anyone. You're like me. Maybe we were meant for each other."

"Chill, baby," Stark cut in. "I don't understand your kick or how you think or what you want. You're in some kind of twilight zone all your own. One minute you act like I'm some kind of shit and you're the Virgin Mary. The next minute you want to get as deep in the gutter with me as you can. I don't understand, but it doesn't matter one way or another. You're here and I dig you. Love isn't in this equation. Momo doesn't know you're with me, so you can stay. Just do what I tell you and stay out of sight for a few days until I can wrap this all up. Then we are out of here. Where's your clothes?"

"I only had a few things. I left them. I just split when he wasn't looking."

Stark nodded, glanced at his watch on the nightstand. "It's getting late. I've got a heavy day tomorrow. Come over here." His voice thickened with meaning. Dorie understood his look and smiled. She unbuttoned the front of her white blouse and took off her bra. Her soft white breasts peeked teasingly from the open garment. Then she crawled along the bed until she was lying beside him. Their mouths met and her tongue explored his. When they ended the kiss she pressed his head down to her tits. He nibbled on them and felt the nipples rising to hardness against his teeth. She arched her back, combed her fingers through his hair and pulled him closer. She began to whimper and whisper, "Do me. Hurt me."

When Stark awoke this morning it was not with the suddenness of other times. He felt logy and had to focus. His body hinted at the need for drugs, and his first thought was for a get-up shot. Then he became aware of the sleeping figure beside him, blankets drawn over her head. She was hell in bed, he thought, smiling faintly. Quietly disentangling himself, he picked up his shorts from where they had been discarded on the carpet, and moved toward the bathroom. He took half his morning fix, trying to cut back, and left enough capsules for Dorie to fix twice; she would need one when she woke and another later in the day. He would be gone until evening, would supply himself and bring some back while moving, but she would be alone. He hoped there was some food around. He was not comfortable with any responsibility for someone else. Through the window the sky was a grey shroud from the sea mist. It was a high overcast, but it kept him from guessing the time. It could be anytime between dawn and eleven-thirty. With sudden anxiety he found his wristwatch and checked it. It was only a few minutes after eight, earlier than he usually got up. His plans had caused him to come awake.

He shaved in the shower while the water pelted him. After deodorant and cologne the scent of her was gone. He slipped into doeskin slacks and hung a shirt and sweater from a doorknob. Dorie was still sleeping, and he decided

STARK

to make the first telephone call before she got up. On tip-toe, he left the bedroom, making certain she hadn't moved before gently closing the door.

There was a growing knot of tension in his belly as he dialed. This was the first cast of the dice, in a calculated parlay gamble.

"Talk smooth, Mr. Slick," he muttered to himself as the receiver began its rhythmic buzzing.

"Oceanview Police," a female operator answered.

"Let me have Lieutenant Crowley's extension."

"One moment, please."

There was a click and another buzzing. Then Stark heard the receiver rise.

"Narcotics Division, Lieutenant Crowley."

"Ernie Stark, boss..."

"Stark," spluttered Crowley; Stark could visualize the blotchy reddening of the policeman's face. "I know all about it," Crowley seethed. "Wilson called me last night. I told him what a rat you are and advised him not to trust you. I want you to know that. But he insisted, so you're free... for now. Are you happy, punk? Your info caused the death of a cop. Forget the bad guys you ratted out."

"Look, lieutenant, it wasn't like you think. It wasn't a game. But you were too impatient, put too much pressure on me. I didn't want you to put the heat on me. I know you've got the upper hand. I'm sorry about the dead cop."

"I'll bet you are. You'll know it better when Wilson gets tired of your bullshit, and I get back in the act. You're gonna know it from the jail ward in the hospital.

141

When I think about you, I wish I could get my hands on you. You're the rottenest excuse for a human being I ever met."

Stark held the phone away from his ear and listened to the tirade of contempt with an expression of wry boredom on his face. When it began to subside, he brought up the mouthpiece.

"Let me say something," he said forcefully, then dripped solemn sincerity into his voice. "I can understand why you despise me. I'm not much good –"

"Not any good."

"Maybe I'm a junkie and a con man. I'll probably always be a hustler. I've tried to quit, and I'm trying to cut back on the shit. You know how this shit drives a guy. It makes him do things that aren't right. I'm not any good, but I'm better than the vultures who peddle it and suck my blood. I hate them as much as you do. I didn't go to Wilson to duck out on you, but like I said, you weren't using any discretion. You despise me so much that you were going to get me killed."

He paused for a response. There was only a grunt. At least it was not ear-burning vilification.

"I'm still working on what you want, and I think I've got an angle."

"Yeah, what's that?"

"I'm pretty sure I can find out who the connection is, if you help me."

"Help you?" Crowley was instantly wary. It edged the tone of his reply. "How's that? Say it real slow, so I can think about it. You are such a slimy rat."

"Momo's shacking up with a young broad."

"I know. Dorie Williams. Age twenty-seven. Good family. No arrest record, but she's an addict. She's a psych case, too. I checked on her with the hospital. See, I know a little about what's going on."

"That's her. The thing is that she goes for me in a big way. She knows who the Man is." He stopped, waiting.

After a few seconds of silence, Crowley snapped, "So pump her. What's that got to do with me? You think I should pick her up and rough her up, or something? They'd have my badge."

"No, not that. I wanna work on her, but I don't get more than a few minutes at a time. Momo's always bird dogging the scene. He don't give her no air. He's the problem. If you could jerk him in for a few hours –" Stark heard the bedroom door click open and broke off. He was on the sofa and cupped the receiver and looked over his shoulder at the girl. She looked curiously at him, but he could tell that she hadn't heard anything. His first impulse was to order her back to the bedroom, but it might create a situation. He decided the conversation could be fogged up at this point so she would not understand the gist of it. He motioned her to go into the kitchen and make him some coffee, holding out his empty hand as if it held a mug he kept sipping.

"Stark… Stark, what the hell," Crowley was angrily shouting.

"Yeah, I'm here."

"Where the hell did you go?"

"A cigarette fell out of the ashtray on the carpet."

"So finish," Crowley pressed.

"If you do what I said, I can make that move and help you. I'm working on that other for Wilson, too."

Crowley sucked his teeth, considering. "All of a sudden you're co-operative as hell."

"You got it wrong. All of a sudden there's something I can do without getting killed. This is good, you might get a promotion out of it."

"Yeah, maybe," Crowley said dubiously. "It might be the truth, and it might be some kind of game." Crowley hesitated, reflected. Stark waited. Finally the cop said, "If it is a game, I can't figure out your angle. But I don't know, you probably have one. I don't have anything to lose, so I'll go for it. When do you want me to take him in? Maybe he'll spill about the connection, then I won't need you."

"Not likely, or you would have done it a long time ago. Do it at noon today, give or take an hour. It shouldn't be too hard."

"No, I can find him by his smell. How long do you want me to hold him?"

"Three or four hours. You can tell him the girl gave up his connection."

"And while he's gone you're gonna lay her."

"That's part of the game... the fun part."

"Will she tell you who the Man is?" asked the cop.

"I know I can get it out of her."

"Oh, Christ! I don't know why I'm a cop. I get dirty just from being around people like you."

"So quit."

"Nope. It's stale, but somebody's got to do it. I got a stronger stomach than most."

"So, I can count on you doing that?"

"Yes. Call me later and tell me what you find out. It better be good, or you're dead meat."

"Sure. Sure. Don't worry."

"Watch out for Dummy. I don't want you dead before I can squeeze you."

"Some joke, Pat," he said and hung up laughing before Crowley could curse him.

There was a grin on his lean face as he turned to Dorie. The girl was still standing near the bedroom door. She was barefoot, wearing only lace panties and the shirt he had discarded the night before. The ensemble accentuated her full, long legs, smooth and firm. Coupled with the lack of makeup and sleep-tousled hair, her appearance was of both extreme youth and lush sensuality. She had a burning cigarette in her mouth and blinked from the rise of smoke. She understood Stark's stare of appraisal and smiled softly. The Veronica Lake look.

"Uh uh," he said. "I've got business this morning."

Dorie shrugged. "Who's Pat? Another girlfriend?"

"Nah, some booster… a deal about some hot merchandise for junk. The guy I was talking to is representing some other sucker. We might burn him. It ain't nothing." He stood up and came around the sofa toward the bedroom. Passing Dorie, he patted her on a bare, warm thigh. "Looking good, baby."

"That'll cost you a fix," she said, "or maybe you want a fuck, too."

"I always like more of you, but I left some shit in the john for you. There's enough for a couple of jolts. I'm trying to cut back. Save some for later. I'll be gone all day."

She nodded, but did not go to the bathroom. For a moment she watched as he began to brush the shoes he was going to wear.

"I'll fix in a few minutes," she said. "I'll make you some coffee if you want."

He nodded absently. "There's a jar of instant in the cupboard. The faucet isn't quite hot enough. Fill a pan and stick it on the stove 'til it boils."

"Jesus, you think I don't know how to make instant coffee?"

Dorie went toward the kitchen. Stark slipped the alligator shoes on and reached for the soft shirt and jacket. He combed his hair into perfect casualness and checked his appearance in the full length mirror on the back of the closet door. He was satisfied. The clothes were expensive and had flair without being flashy. Nobody would guess he was a thief and a con artist. He looked like a husband in suburbia with a ten thousand a year income, and good taste in clothes. Starting to leave, he had an impulse. He took the small automatic and slipped it into his front pocket. It weighed slightly against his leg, but did not bulge his jacket. He went out to the kitchen.

Dorie had not only made the coffee but was just about scrambling bacon and eggs. They sizzled on the small stove. She was crouching down, checking the oven, when he arrived.

"If you wait for this to heat up you can have toast."

"I haven't got time."

"The other stuff will be ready in two minutes."

He grunted, but flickered a smile. He was anxious to get moving and felt strange at this display of thoughtfulness.

"Go sit at the table," she ordered. "I'll bring you the coffee."

He complied, sipped the steamy black liquid, and watched her semi-nude figure swish barefooted back to the stove. "You're too much, Dorie. You blow as many ways as the wind."

"I only feel like this once in a while. Sometimes I go the other way and don't do anything for weeks except lay in bed and wipe out everything with junk."

He sensed something of an appeal on its way, and cut her off. "Just bring my breakfast. Save the history for later," he said somewhat abruptly.

She brought the bacon and eggs. "The refrigerator is empty. The milk's sour and the oranges are green. We should have something to eat if you don't want me to go into town."

"I'll take care of it. You won't starve." He began to eat. She watched for a moment, then indicated she was going to shoot up.

Stark gulped down the meal and kept track of the time. It was five to ten. His show had to get on the road. He went to the bedroom door and leaned inside. Dorie was still in the bathroom.

"I'm leaving, baby," he called. "It'll be a long day. You could go for a swim in the afternoon. It'll get hot later."

Laughter erupted from the bedroom.

"In my bra and panties? They'd arrest me for indecent exposure."

"They might arrest you, but you wouldn't show them anything indecent... not naked. I forgot you didn't bring any clothes." He started to add this to his other problems, but caught himself, and pushed it away. Dorie's lack of clothes could wait. "Goodbye, baby."

"What time are you coming back?"

"Not sure. Maybe five. Don't clock me."

"I'll clean the house today. There's a layer of dust on everything."

"Don't bother. I like it the way it is." Now she wants to set up house? Forget it. He wasn't at all comfortable with this domestic scene. She was moving in too fast for him.

14

The sun was rapidly burning away the gray overcast as Stark entered Oceanview. The tang of the ocean was in the air, even downtown. By noon the city would bask in golden warmth. It was a good day in several ways. Thinking of the scheme in its complexity, he chuckled. It might prove to be a helluva day…

The mood of gaiety was still with him as he parked near Momo's apartment. He even whistled softly as he went up the stairs, though, as he knocked, he composed himself solemnly. This was serious business.

Bearded and unkempt, Momo opened the door. The guy's black hair was a tangle and the only button fastened on his rumpled clothes was the top one of his pants, a concession to keeping them up. There was a stench of booze and his eyeballs were inflamed. On the cigarette-burned table in the middle of the room was an empty fifth of cheap whiskey. Beside it was a similar bottle a third full. There was an ounce package of heroin, broken open roughly, by drunken hands. Some of the white powder was spilled out onto the table. An outfit rested in a glass of water.

Stark scanned all of this as he waited for Momo to close the door behind him. The dumb slob was strung out on the broad and was hurting. She would never get to him that way.

"This is pretty careless," Stark said, waving at the junk. "Leaving that ten-year sentence out there in the open. The heat might bust the door down. Then what?"

Momo waved a hand in a gesture rejecting the advice. He sank down in a chair next to the table and poured a drink. "If they bust the door down, then I guess I'd do that ten years." He tossed the whiskey down and eyed Stark from head to toe.

"You're lookin' pretty sharp today, as usual. Who was that guy in England who was the famous sharp dresser? Couple hundred years ago, I guess?"

"Beau Brummel."

"Yeah, that's you. Big Beau. Want a drink?"

Stark accepted, though it was still morning.

"I should start wearing sharp clothes," Momo continued, pouring Stark a drink and another for himself.

"I might have been able to keep my old lady then."

Stark's brow wrinkled with surprise and concern. "What's wrong, man? Where's Dorie?"

"The bitch quit me. Poof." Momo flapped his arms. "She flew the coop, sneaked out last night."

"What'd you do to her? Kick her ass or something?"

Momo managed a sickly laugh. "Kick her ass! Hell no. I was drunk and affectionate when we got home and told her we should get married. Go to Hawaii on our honeymoon. See my folks. She blew her cork. She acted like I'd said something dirty, like she would be going to bed with her father or something. Then I tried to make love to her and she wouldn't let me. I almost whipped her then — wish I had — but I decided to get really drunk instead. When I was gone to buy liquor, she took off. The door was open and she was gone without taking her clothes or anything. No note. Nothing. For a while I thought she just went out for a walk to cool off or something, but she went farther than that. I hunted the neighborhood till three this morning. I know she didn't hook up with you. She kept telling me to watch out for you. That you were evil. Dames. How can you figure them?" Momo tossed his shoulders at the futility of it.

"She might come back. She's hooked, and she'll need some stuff."

"She can always get somebody to give her stuff, fine as she is." Momo raised his glass, stared at its empty depths in the timeworn pose of reflection, and began to muse in a soft, whiskey-thickened voice. "I guess I loved her. She's nuts, and a squarejohn broad, but she's got a sharp mind. But she could run hot and then, suddenly, cold." Momo shook his head slowly. Without warning, he drew back his arm and hurled the glass against a wall. It shattered. Startled, Stark jumped.

"Man, be cool. It's only pussy. You knew she was nuts. You may be better off."

Momo glared at him on the edge of violence.

"Don't blow it," Stark admonished calmly. "I'm your partner and your friend. I wouldn't come between you and her. I know how you felt. Maybe she'll stroll back in after she's cooled off. You never know about dames. On the other hand, this may be a good thing for you. The broad is wacky and knows too much. What would've happened if they'd pulled her in and put the heat on her? She'd have given us both up. We're better off without her."

"Maybe you're right, but..."

"So is a broad worth a trip to prison?" Stark shook his head in disgust. "Man, when we set this up, we can have really fine broads, those stylish bitches you see in magazines. We'll have so much money... and you'll be in a Caddy..." Stark drew a brief verbal picture of how they would live. His voice rang with glib optimism. Momo listened and calmed down somewhat.

"You're right, I know that. But she had me hooked real good. I'll be okay. I can see things like they really are and I'll take care of business." Momo even managed a grin of assurance, not wanting his associate to wonder if he was buckling under pressure. "You're a good partner. You're smarter than me. I know that. Maybe that's why I didn't like you for so long. I thought you was lookin' down on me like I was a fool or something. And Dummy said not to trust you."

Stark threw back his head and laughed. "Hell, I didn't like you 'cause you had all the junk. I was jealous. But forget all that. It's nothing." He cuffed Momo on the shoulder. "Let's get this junk out of sight and get down to business. Leave out seven or eight grams. I might make that run to Riverside today and get rid of them... set up that pusher, too."

Five minutes later, the heroin was hidden in a drain-pipe just outside the bathroom window. The pipe had been plugged at the roof so nothing could come down. The package was hung on a wire at a joint that could be disconnected, but if the disconnection was not made in a certain way, after a pencil or knife blade was inserted into a hole a few inches below, the package would fall free down the pipe. Only Stark, Momo and Dorie knew the combination. It was easy to get at and almost impossible for police to find; if they did find it, the odds against own-ership being proven in court were tremendous.

Together Stark and Momo partially straightened the dreary quarters. The bed was made, floor swept, and the bottles thrown into the wastebasket. Dirty clothes were piled in the bathtub as there was no laundry hamper. Stark took out the garbage while Momo went to shave. He was still shaving when Stark came back, entered the bath-room, and sat down on the toilet lid, leaning back in a comfortable semi-prone position. In the wastebasket were all of Dorie's cosmetics.

"You ought to move out of this hole," Stark said. "You've got enough money already."

"I should, but —" he shrugged. "It's better'n what I was raised in. On the island, my whole family slept in one small room. The toilet was an outhouse in the back."

"I didn't grow up in Beverly Hills either. But I got a nice little apartment, real modern."

Momo paused the razor in midstroke. "Yeah, by the way, where is your place? It ain't in the tenderloin or I'd know it. I wondered about that yesterday."

"It's over in that new apartment house area near Broadcrest," he lied. "I'll take you over in a couple days. Maybe tomorrow. In fact, tomorrow we're gonna get you some clothes and find you an apartment in a better neighborhood. This place is too hot. The cops are always around and know where to find you. Too many junkies have your address. That's dangerous."

Momo finished with the razor and, without a rinse, wiped off the remaining bits of lather with a towel, discarding that into the bathtub. "You should give me your phone number so I can get to you if something important happens."

"I will when I get one. They should put it in next week. I've been waiting for a month."

"They usually put them in quick."

"Maybe they goofed or something. It's a new apartment building and the other people got theirs. I'll call the company tomorrow."

Momo accepted the lie without suspicion and went into the other room. Before following, Stark checked the time. It was ten minutes to eleven. He walked out of the bathroom directly toward the front door, stopping just in front of it.

"I better get moving."

"What's the hurry? Stick around. Go to breakfast with me."

"I ate already. It's a long drive to Riverside, better than two hours. I don't want it to be dark when I get there and I've got to hunt a guy down. Anyway, there's no money just bullshitting with you. Nothing we could do together that you can't handle alone."

Momo smiled sheepishly. "You're right again. I can sell dope in Oceanview without any help. I just wanted some company."

"I'll be back about four o'clock. What're you gonna do?"

"After I get breakfast I'll get a haircut – first step on the new, suave Momo Mendoza. Then I'll do what I always do, take some junk down to the Panama. They'll be waiting for me with their noses running and half of 'em will be a dollar short."

"I'll meet you at the club about four. If I can't make it until later I'll telephone and let you know. Remember, tomorrow we're going shopping for your wardrobe. When I get you elegant, I might even get you some sweet young broad… if you promise not to fall in love." Stark waved goodbye and went out before Momo could reply.

The station wagon covered two blocks swiftly and was parked beside a telephone booth. He dialed the number of the Oceanview Police. The same operator buzzed the extension.

"Narco Division, Crowley."

"Look, boss. I just left Momo at his pad. He's going out for breakfast in a few minutes. He'll eat in the neighborhood. Then he's gonna get a haircut. After that he'll make his usual run to the Panama Club. That's the best time to get him, on the way, so no hustler sees what's happening. The broad might find out and go on a panic. You know she's not right upstairs. Get the idea?"

Crowley did not seem enthused. "Yeah, okay."

"You're gonna do it, aren't you?"

"I said I was."

"You don't seem happy about it."

"It's just my job, a dirty part of it. I get paid and do it as best I can. You think I should jump up and down about scheming with the enemy?"

"Okay," Stark said, understanding the attitude. "But there's one more thing. He might have a balloon of junk in his mouth."

"And that's something new for street pushers?" Crowley growled sarcastically.

"No, but tell whoever makes the roust to make sure Momo has enough warning to swallow it. If they got it off him, you'd have to lock him up or it'll look funny. You keep him in the slammer too long, the connection might get worried and disappear. This has got to look like questioning about something. I know you can find something still on the books. Then let him out about five."

"I know how it's got to look. What the hell! You ain't only finking, you're trying to run my job. I never saw a stool pigeon so worried or so enthusiastic." The contempt in Pat Crowley's voice caused Stark to redden with anger, yet he managed to continue the servility and the nervousness act.

"I'm just trying to make sure it goes right, to protect myself. My neck is out. Man, you almost got my head blown off with that last uncool move."

Crowley didn't answer.

"Lieutenant?" he queried, wondering if they had been disconnected.

"Maybe your pal, the fat Hawaiian, will give me the name of his supplier. Then I won't have to chase you. I'll just let Dummy know you are ratting out all your friends."

"That's not funny, I'm trying to help you."

The receiver went dead.

Mute fury burned as he climbed behind the wheel. He wished there was a way to destroy the cop. Maybe a slick frame-up... But there were more immediate things to consider. He checked the gas gauge. A fill-up was needed for the long drive. He had a couple of stops to make in Riverside and then south to an exclusive suburb of La Jolla.

15

The night before, he'd called up Alfie to set up a meeting with the local Mex drug dealer. He told his friend he had a plan that would make him rich and eliminate the competition.

"You're not going to kill the guy, are you?" Alfie asked. "That would be nuts."

"No, calm your engine," Stark responded. "This is strictly a business deal."

Stark needed to get to the top guy in the Mex network, to see if they would be interested in his higher class shit. He had a plan that would put him in the driver's seat and make him rich.

The Mexican was waiting beside his rusty pickup truck. Nothing flashy that might attract attention. Every Mex drove one of these wanted to keep a low profile. The Chicanos with their souped-up low-riders were always eyed by the cops.

The pusher was huge, dark-skinned, his features Indian. Another big Mex was with him. The other guy looked like he was carrying heat. The bodyguard said nothing, his contempt for the two gringos apparent from the first moment. The dealer spoke only a few words, sprinkled frequently with obscenities. He was both surly and suspicious when he learned they were not buyers, but sellers.

Ten minutes later, the atmosphere had changed – not to friendliness, but to uncertainty. Stark gave him a liberal sample of the high grade heroin taken from the drainpipe in Momo's flat a few hours earlier. Stark told him to show it to his boss and promised to deliver an unlimited supply at a price that was almost ridiculous. The offer was so good that the Mexican's eyes widened in wonder. Later, Stark explained to Alfie that after the first delivery, they would start to jack up their prices. Stark was sure that greed would bring his boss forward for a meet. The fear would come from someone who wanted to buy, not someone who wanted to sell. The Mex would call Alfie to set up the meet with his boss.

It was early afternoon and heat waves shimmered above the asphalt when Stark drove slowly past the Aztec Travel Agency. It was in a long, one storey building, new and white, its front window showing colorful travel posters with the names of faraway places and Greyhound, TWA, BOAC, and others. He turned at the corner and circled through the alley at the rear, noting a back door to the agency. Beside it, in a parking slot, was a new Cadillac.

He parked in a lot half a block away and walked down the boulevard, stopping at the window as if to scrutinize the charts with rates for tours and their schedules. But he was really checking inside, where there were two employees – a kid and a dame, both in their twenties, clean cut, collegiate. They couldn't be involved in the wholesaling of junk. They were busy at desks and did not look up. He loitered inconspicuously and finally was rewarded. From a door at the rear marked 'Private,' a middle-age woman appeared. She was dressed expensively, with neatly done gray hair and lots of gold jewelry. She talked to the two kids, picked up some papers, and went back to her office. It all looked legit. Maybe he'd made a mistake.

Stark turned away. He'd have to wait it out for the Man to arrive. Across the street was a coffee shop with a good view of the travel agency. He ordered a cuppa, grabbed a window seat and made himself comfortable. He started to worry, maybe Momo was giving up the name of his supplier. If so, cop cars would be swarming the place, soon enough.

After an hour of waiting, he had just about decided to brace the place when a familiar convertible pulled into the curb across the street. It was Dummy. He watched as the mute rushed inside. The door marked 'Private' opened. A few minutes later, Dummy came out, the old dame walking him to the door. Under his arm, he carried a small parcel. Stark could guess what was in the package. Momo told him he was a runner.

As soon as Dummy drove away, Stark left the table and crossed the street. Maybe the Man, himself, was still inside. Inside the travel agency, the air-conditioned coolness chilled him. The girl rose from her desk and came forward. She was tan and wholesome, with a zestful prettiness born of youth and health. She smiled, her teeth perfect.

"I'm planning a three-month vacation for me and my wife. Is the boss in? I'd like to get some ideas of costs and plan an itinerary."

"Well, we have a number of travel brochures I can give you..."

"Nah, let me talk to your boss."

"I'll see if Mrs. Klein is available. Who should I say you are?"

"My name is Burdman."

She left him to knock on the door of the inner office and went in.

He looked around while he waited. The young man was at a desk, writing diligently. Except for a glance, he had not paid any attention to him.

The agency was small, but it was a going business, not just a front. He had expected at least one shady character, or something undercover. If it hadn't been for the visit from Dummy, he would have thought he was on the wrong track.

The girl beckoned him, still smiling. "All right, Mr. Burdman. Mrs. Klein will see you now."

The girl announced him, then faded inconspicuously out, as the woman came around her desk to offer her hand. She smiled, but Stark could see there was no warmth as her cold eyes checked him out.

"Mr. Burdman, nice to meet you. Why don't you sit down. I understand you and your wife are planning a long trip. How can I help you?"

Their hands met.

"I'm actually here to meet Mr. Klein. Is he around? I have some private business to discuss with him."

"I'm afraid you'll have a long wait, Mr. Burdman. You see, my husband passed away three years ago. I've been running the agency ever since."

"A fellow I know advised me to come here – Momo Mendoza."

"I'm sorry, but I don't recognize the name."

"You know him. He's a very fat Hawaiian drug dealer. You couldn't forget him. He's probably the only Hawaiian dealer in California. You sold him some very good drugs lately."

"I think you've made a mistake. I know no such person. We are a licensed travel agency and have been in business for fifteen years."

"No deal, lady. I just saw your runner, my pal, Dummy, leave your place. That was no stack of travel brochures he was carrying under his arm."

"Do you mean Mr. Floyd? He is a messenger for our

EDWARD BUNKER

best clients. He usually hand delivers airplane tickets and reservations to our good customers. There's nothing illegal here. Who are you, the police? Show me your I.D."

"Let's stop kidding each other. I came here to do you a favor. That is, if Momo is not spilling his guts to the cops as we talk. They picked him up a couple of hours ago. Momo and I are partners. He told me you are his connection – except he called you the Man."

"If you don't leave immediately, I will call the police. I know a shakedown when I see it. And I know an ex-convict when I meet one. The cops will be happy to take you in on my complaint."

"Now, let's not get too hasty. I came to do you a favor. A big favor. I happen to know that your biggest competitor, the Mexican network, will soon be out of business. With the high quality of dope you have, we can take their place. They dealt mostly with Mexicans, but my partner, Momo, can take over that action. I have connections that are ready to fall into place."

"Who else knows you've come here?" she asked, a bit more interested. "Who told you about me?"

"My partner, Momo, but he kept calling you the Man. I guess he wanted to throw me off."

"This Momo character says he's met me?"

"Of course."

Mrs. Klein laughed. "No dealer has ever met me. Except one guy, and Mr. Floyd, the man you call Dummy, took care of that problem. How do I know you're not a cop? How do I know that everything you have told me is not a lie?"

"Ask Dummy if he doesn't know me. We go back to our shared time, courtesy of the State. We're pals. He can vouch for me."

"Did *he* tell you about me?"

"Not likely. They don't call him Dummy because he can't talk. They call him that because he *won't* talk."

"So how did you find me?"

"Dummy should not carry around your travel agency matches. That, and the fact that Momo knew the connection was in La Jolla. I just added the two pieces of info together. Dummy's visit today cinched things."

"Who else knows about me?"

"Well, I'm going to have to tell my partner, Momo, but he won't talk. He'd be afraid of Dummy."

"How do I know I can trust you? Why should I?"

"You'll need me. We need each other. There's millions lying out there for the taking."

"Give me twenty-four hours to think about this. I'm not sure I can handle the supply for a big expansion of the business. I'm not sure I want to. I do all right as it is."

"If we don't move in now, someone else will, and they won't want your competition. It's now or never."

"Let me think about it. Give me a number where I can reach you. I have to see if I can or want to take this on. In the meantime, forget you have ever been here. And don't tell anyone. Not if you want to live."

"I don't have a phone number for you, but Dummy

knows how to find me. Or Momo. If I don't hear from you in twenty-four hours, a certain narcotics detective will be hearing about our meeting."

"No need to threaten me. You have no proof. Even now. Don't cross me, or you'll hear a different tune from Mr. Floyd. Am I making myself clear?"

"Now, let's try to be nice, here. Neither of us wants to go to prison – not while we're about to begin a very profitable relationship. I'll await your call."

Mrs. Klein shook his outstretched hand. A good sign that a deal was in the making. He couldn't wait to tell Momo that the Man was a woman. What a kick.

"You can find your way out, I suppose, Mr. Burdman? That's not your real name, is it? If we are going to be partners, I should know your real name. What is it?"

"Just call me Stark. That will do."

"Good day, Mr. Stark. You'll hear from me."

Stark left the agency, walked down the block. The street was on fire. Going from the refrigerator of the agency to an oven outside was like being hit over the head by a hammer. He found a phone booth and rang Momo's joint. He should be out of the slammer by now.

The phone rang and rang. There was no answer. Momo couldn't still be in jail. He couldn't have given up his connection to Crowley. He didn't know it was a woman. Could the cop be sweating him out, like he did Stark? He'd call again when he got to Oceanview.

As he drove home, he wondered if he had taken the right approach. This Mrs. Klein was no rube. In fact, she was dangerous. The wrong move and she'd have him in the slammer, or dead. He wouldn't be able to con her. He had to figure out a way to get his network up and running as soon as she gave him a green light. How was he going to do this? And how was he going to break the news to Momo – especially about Dorie? He would have to get rid of the dame. He needed Momo more. She'd survive.

16

The last red light of day was on Oceanview as Stark entered the Panama Club. The action was slow at that hour. The two bartenders, already on duty, were stocking their wares and mixes. The 'B' girls sat in a gaudy row on the stools, three magpies, chewing gum and chattering. A handful of customers were at the bar. The jukebox was temporarily silent.

"You're on the scene early, honey," one of the girls commented.

"Might catch a live one, pretty. The early bird catches the worm." Stark started toward a vacant stool at the rear. Then he stopped. "Elaine, you seen Momo?"

The girl looked back to Stark. She noted his haggard appearance and misjudged its origin. "No, baby. I don't think he's been in all day. Some other people were askin' for him, earlier. They didn't look good. Jess made them leave."

He nodded. "Thanks. I just wanted to see him. Buy him a drink." He went to the stool, thinking; Crowley had fulfilled his mission, but where was Momo? Stark would have to telephone the cop to find out what was happening. He needed Momo for their new expansion, but the cop wouldn't rest until he had someone in the bag. How to keep out of jail and make the deal work – right under his nose? Now that would be his biggest con – if he could get away with it. He'd need to throw him someone. Soon.

The bartender appeared, also commenting on his early arrival. He shrugged and forced himself to be garrulous.

"Nothing else is happening. I thought I might come in and hook up with one of the girls early before she gets busy. I might even spend some money with her." He winked meaningfully, and the bartender laughed.

"Got one of them in mind?"

"It's all the same, ain't it. Looks the same in the dark."

"You ought to try out that new little Oriental. I went out with her a couple of nights ago. She's got it good."

"I might just do that. I was looking her over last night. Gimme a double shot of Harper's. Get yourself a drink, too." He brought out a thick wad of green. "I'm loaded."

One thing Crowley might go for would be to pull

down the whole Mexican network. Alfie, at their meet in Santa Ana, had given him the name of the Mex who delivered in this area. Probably an illegal. Once Crowley got the guy, he could sweat him with deportation. That might keep him busy and give him and Momo a chance to move in.

He went to the phone outside the men's room and called Momo's number. "Hello?"

Shit, it was Dorie.

"What the fuck are you doing in Momo's pad? I told you to stay low. You're going to queer my deal with Momo. Are you nuts?"

"I couldn't stay at your place. About an hour ago the phone rang. I answered it, but no one said anything. Fifteen minutes later, the phone rang again. I thought it was you and told you to fuck off. It wasn't you that called, was it?"

"No, I didn't call. Somebody must be playing games." Could Klein have made up her mind so soon?

"Well, it creeped me out. I came back to Momo's place, but he's not here. I suppose he's with you at the club."

"No, he ain't here. Where the fuck can he be? He's got customers looking for him here, too. You might as well stay where you are. Momo don't have to know where you slept last night. Give him some bullshit story. You're good at that. I told him you were out cooling off and might come back. I'll call you back soon as he shows up."

He hung up and then dialed Crowley's number.

"Let me speak to Lieutenant Crowley."

EDWARD BUNKER

"He's out of the office. Who's calling?"

"The name's Stark."

"He left word that he needed to speak to you urgently. Please leave your number, and he'll call you as soon as he gets in."

"I'm not leaving any number. I'll call you back in an hour."

Over a double shot of bourbon, Stark thought of how all the pieces were falling into place. He would get rid of the Mex network with just one call to a forever grateful Crowley. He called Momo's apartment again, but Dorie said he still hadn't shown. She sounded scared. He was at a point of emotional saturation. So much treachery in so little time had exhausted his capacity for stimulation. He did not feel tension as he glanced at his watch. He just wondered if Momo was okay.

After another double shot, the bourbon began to take effect. Anxiety started to fade away. His eyes roamed over the garish confines of the club, now filling with its usual crowd. Without consciously looking for her, he found himself focusing on the Asian-American mentioned by the bartender; she was the same girl Dummy had stared at the evening before. She was beautiful, small and perfectly proportioned, and seemed very young. By some strange alchemy, the mixture of blood created an aura similar to that exuded by Dorie, of sensuality and innocence. Her raven tresses were pulled back from high cheekbones and knotted in a bun, accentuating the pixie face and almond eyes. At the moment, her head was cocked to one side in

172

a quizzical pose as she listened to an older hustler. Her almond-shaped eyes met Stark's.

Stark caught the glance of the bartender and beckoned him. "You know that little broad, huh?"

"Which one?"

"The little doll down there. The one we were talking about."

"Oh, yeah, Toy. If you wanna meet her, she's on the market."

"Has she got an old man?"

"No. She's an outlaw. Plenty are making plays for her, though."

"I'll bet. What did you say her name was?"

"Toy."

"That fits her. Tell her to come on down. I wanna buy her a drink."

The bartender nodded, and started away.

"Toy," muttered Stark, watching the girl as the bartender motioned her to lean close. With Dorie having left, he might need a new girlfriend with no complications. Certainly, she was the most attractive babe in the neighborhood. He tossed down the remains of his drink and watched the girl walk toward him.

There was an uncommon grace about her, provocative without the blatancy of most of the streetwalking breed. Her smile, when she reached Stark, was professionally impish and jaded. She took in his slight intoxication from the glaze of his eyes.

"You wanted to see me about something?" The way she

said it was not a question; it was both a challenge and an invitation.

"I just wanted to talk a little bit."

The smile faded slightly. "Time is money, honey."

"I know. Mine's real valuable."

The smile was gone, replaced by perplexity. She did not speak for a long time, nor could her thoughts be read in the blackness of her eyes.

"So?" she asked finally.

"Sit down and have a drink." He waved toward a stool.

She looked at the stool, then back at him. He knew she was wondering if he was naive or joking.

He grinned and brought out the fat roll of bills. "I'm not usually a john, pretty, but tonight I'm a little lushed, I'm rich, so what's the fee for conversation?"

Toy glanced nervously around the room to see if there were any vice officers to note the flash of green. She hesitated, then perched on a stool.

"Put it away. Talk costs only a drink. Anything else — we'll talk about it then. You seem to know the game."

"Baby, I'm the one that originated the game."

Toy smiled at his boast.

"So what can I buy you?"

"Screwdriver."

He snapped his fingers for the bartender and ordered for her and a refill for himself.

"Don't lose any money on account of me, baby," he said. "If a live one shows up, take care of business." He winked. She blushed. "It's nice you can do that," he said.

"Blush, I mean. You're not as tough as you act."

"We'll see how tough if someone walks in."

"You do what you have to do. That's taking care of business." He laughed and she joined him. The smile lines made her look like a young, innocent kid. "They call you Toy. What's your last name?"

"O'Neill."

"Toy O'Neill. That's a gas. Real professional, like Suzy Wong or something." He looked at her glistening eyes, the pureness of her skin. "You're a doll, baby, a real swinger."

"So are you. You sure know how to talk the talk." But she glowed with stimulation.

"That's me, beautiful. Ernie Stark, con man, gambler, and the world's foremost talker. But you almost leave me speechless. I might even spend some money and time with you."

She laughed. "You're too much."

"Tell me about yourself."

"About myself. What do you want, the sordid story of how some man done me wrong and now I want to get revenge on men? Or how I was tricked into this?"

"Tell me anything. A good lie is better than the dull truth."

"One thing, don't give me the old bit about how I ought to find a man, get married, and settle down and raise children."

"Baby," Stark said, feigning hurt indignation. "I would never tell you that. I'm not the marrying kind myself. Love 'em and leave 'em. This is the crazy life, fast and dangerous. I love it." The bartender brought their drinks. He paid and picked his up. "In fact, let's drink to the way we live. It might not last long, but who cares?" Stark tossed down the double shot in two quick gulps and immediately looked for the bartender.

Toy O'Neill was fascinated by Stark; she watched him with a smile etched on her face. He looked back to her, and now he had a serious expression.

"What happens when you're not young and pretty?"

"I thought you said 'who cares?'"

"That was minutes ago. I'm liable to say anything."

"It'll be a long time. I'm only twenty."

"Twenty. Damn, you ain't even supposed to be in here drinking."

"You're not serious." Then she saw the gleam of laughter and reached out to playfully slap his wrist. "Quit it."

"Seriously, where'd you come from? You're new here."

"I'm on parole from the state school for girls."

"They didn't parole you to do this."

"No. They paroled me to be a waitress in a hash joint in downtown L.A."

"You're better off here. Oceanview's all right. It's small and there's not too much competition for the action. You get to know who's who and this and that. I do all right."

"You must — if that roll of money means anything. What's your hustle? It's not from an old lady, is it?"

He made a derogatory gesture with his hand. "No broad can make as much as me. They can't stand the pace. I move, baby. I keep it on the road." There was a surge of glibness and a feeling of power; the bragging in hip phrases was the truth at this moment – his truth. "Me, I'm king of everything... 'cause I'm cold, baby, because I'm slick and I'm cold. I do what I want and I don't feel a thing. If anybody gets in my way, I jerk their legs out – they know something bad happened, but they don't know how. The bankroll is fat now, but in a week or so I'm gonna have a lot more. I might even buy this joint. I've got something going..." He let the story trail off without giving any details; despite the whiskey, he was too well trained to spill too much.

Toy was curious; it showed in her wrinkled forehead and the way she leaned closer. But she was well enough versed in the ways of guys with fat rolls of dough who knew the game that she did not press for information.

He talked on, saying nothing, just liking to hear himself. He was alternately flattering to Toy and boastful about himself. The monologue had a twang of humor, just enough to hide the ego. It kept the girl giggling and fascinated.

The conversation was interrupted by the bartender, who summoned Toy aside and whispered that a big money trick was at the other end of the bar. Toy came back and looked to Stark with apology. She explained the situation and finished, "A girl has to make a living."

She waited for comment. He was now bleary-eyed and did not notice her pause for his approval.

"No problem?" she finally asked.

"A girl's got to take care of business. Business always

comes first." He laughed and winked.

She slid off the stool. "When will I see you? Later tonight?"

Stark looked at her pretty face, not yet hardened. She would be good. "Tomorrow. I might even fill your whole dance card, if things go right."

"You don't have to," she said quietly.

He blinked, realizing that she had propositioned him. Before he could put the idea together, Toy was gone. He watched her wiggle down the bar. "Damn," he muttered. "I am sharp. I caught the finest whore on the scene without trying." He gloated about the offer and then remembered to look at the time. It was nine-thirty. Without emotion, he realized that it was time to telephone Crowley and find out what he was so hot about. Was he still holding Momo? He glanced at Toy flirting with the trick. Tomorrow he would see her. They had a date. He pushed himself away from the bar and moved uncertainly toward the door. Around him the Panama Club was in full swing. The broken-souled people laughed to tears, the music throbbed, the smoke was thick.

17

With the coming of night, a chill fog had rolled into Oceanview. It pressed the glow of the street lamps back against the bulbs and blurred the outlines of the buildings and parked cars. There was no breeze, but the air was damp and cold against his cheeks. He breathed deeply and closed his eyes, trying to clear his head. The sounds from the club grew dimmer as he walked toward the station wagon around the corner. He had a slight headache and his stomach was queasy. As soon as the phone call to Crowley was finished, a fix was in order. That opiate would take care of all the pain.

He turned the corner and saw his car at the curb two

blocks away. The side street was dimmer and empty of traffic. Only the shadowy figure of a heavy-set dark faced guy was visible, across the street from his car.

He saw an automobile approaching through the fog. As it came abreast of the stranger, there was a series of loud backfires. They exploded loudly and reverberated against the walls of the surrounding buildings. The sound was familiar. Shots. He was twenty yards from the guy, who was now moving in his direction. He felt as though he was just watching the scene play out, and yet, even through the haze of bourbon, reality registered on him. Something electric coursed through him. Someone was shooting at him. This guy didn't look like Dummy, he was moving too slowly. Had Mrs. Klein sent him? Was this her answer?

Without hesitation, Stark stepped between two automobiles and out onto the asphalt. The instantaneous fear verged on panic. He moved across the street, glancing back toward the sidewalk. The figure turned between two other cars to intercept him. He spun back, and sprinted, back in the general direction he had come from.

The noise of heavy-footed steps came from the fog behind him. He almost cried out and hurried his pace. The thudding steps sounded closer. He looked back just as the revolver flashed a tongue of fire and the report came at him simultaneously. A piece of brick from the wall beside him kicked off against his cheek. Two more shots followed in almost one explosion.

Terror made his legs fly. He reached the corner of the

main street and turned right, hurtling down the sidewalk, then ducking to the left between other parked cars and continuing down the asphalt, keeping the steel bodies between him and the bullets.

No more shots followed him, though every muscle was tensed for the impact. He reached the next intersection and glanced back as he turned another corner. The street was empty. On the next block there was a crowd of people beneath the light of the Panama Club door, drawn by the sound of gunfire. He had the urge to slip back into the protection of the crowd, but he knew there was no real safety there. Death might be lurking in the shadows, might be anywhere. He turned left again, running for half a block and then turning into a driveway. The gravel crunched loudly, seeming to scream his whereabouts.

The driveway led to an old frame apartment house with a row of locked garages and a dirt yard. The yard was bounded by a high board fence. Stark came up to the barrier and spun around, heart pounding, eyes wild. He was trapped, afraid to climb the fence and enter the alley beyond, afraid of what might be lurking there. Through the drifting fog he saw a row of trash barrels beside the looming shape of an incinerator. Panting and whimpering, he stumbled over and crouched down behind them, staring out at the mouth of the driveway. The street lamps made the driveway a lighter gray.

His senses were keyed to hear the sound of feet, to see the figure rise up. But nothing moved, only the swirling fog. There was silence except for faint strains of radio music from somewhere in the apartment house, and the occasional swoosh of an automobile passing. Once, a car came slowly down the alley, its headlights splashing through the cracks in the fence. He cowered farther down, wondering if the unseen driver was the mute.

The minutes ticked into half an hour. His pounding heartbeat and blind terror slowly subsided. He was afraid of leaving, but clung to his temporary safety. He sat down and extended his legs, relieving the muscle ache. An itch on his face caused him to scratch, and he discovered a dried rivulet of blood running to his chin. It was a cut from the chip of brick. Dampening his handkerchief on his tongue, he wiped away the blood, then trembled with the awareness of how near death had come.

"Jesus, that was close," he muttered, the sound of his voice seeming unreal. He shook his head, began to think…

Klein had marked him for death. This was certain. But why? He tried to imagine where he had slipped and couldn't. He'd given her a terrific deal. Why the cross up? After considering everything he could imagine, he could only conclude that she didn't want to leave anyone alive who could identify her. He thought about it and decided it was the same decision he might have made in a similar predicament; especially to a con man junkie who had come from nowhere and knew too much. Hell, there were a number of things that might have happened, and no way to know which of them was right. Could Momo have found out about him and Dorie or him and Crowley?

The problem now was what to do. Quickly, he ran several alternatives: go to Klein and try to smooth things over; make an anonymous call to the police; or go on the run. These ideas crowded upon each other, and were rejected almost as swiftly. Klein was too dangerous, and she might send another killer to get him. For once, the police were out of the question; even with an anonymous call there would be too much digging and too many things might come out. He was fucked.

The only thing to do was disappear. Klein could not track him in another city, perhaps another state. There might be some hunt by the police, but not much. He could take Dorie with him. Where? San Francisco came to mind. The price of junk in the Bay Area was twice that of Los Angeles. He had almost twelve hundred dollars' worth at those prices, plus the thirteen hundred cash in his pocket. It was a fair bankroll, and Stark knew a madame with a whorehouse in the Napa Valley where Dorie could be safe. Many of the smaller counties in the northern part of the state had poker rooms he could hustle. He had options. Not many.

Several other places came to mind, but the first choice seemed the best, all things considered.

"Yeah, it's time to blow," he said to himself. Tomorrow morning, in daylight, it would be safe to pick up the station wagon. The neighborhood would be filled with people. What to do until then? How much time did he have?

He lit a cigarette, carefully shielding the match so there was no glare, and went over the situation again. The factor that required special consideration was the police. If they really put out the heat, they would find him. One way to get Crowley off his back would be to call him and give him Klein. He hadn't met the Mex boss, so he couldn't throw him that, as well. He had to find a phone booth.

On the corner, its light casting a weird glow in the fog, was an all-night cigar store. Stark slipped into one of the booths, put his nickel in the slot and rang the police station. He was put through to Crowley immediately.

"Where the fuck are you, you lousy rat?" was his greeting.

"I'll tell you where if you give me a moment to get a word in edgewise. I've been ducking bullets. Someone was shooting at me. I don't think it was Dummy. Some other guy? Who knows about us?"

"Listen, I couldn't care less what happened to you, now that you dumped a murder in my lap."

"What murder? Who got killed?"

"You mean you didn't murder your pal, your partner, Momo?"

"Shit, you're telling me he's dead?"

"You don't know? Now here I'm thinking that you set me up for a patsy. Take Momo in for a few hours. Shake him up. Scare him – all so you can take the afternoon off and fuck his girlfriend. What do I look like to you, a fuckin' pimp?"

"Where was he killed? When?"

"A few hours after I turned him loose, I got a call from some dame. She told me to send an ambulance to his apartment. When we got there, he was dead – and the girlfriend was not around. If you didn't kill him off, maybe she did."

"Dorie is no killer, believe me. She's her own worst enemy. I don't think she'd know how to fire a gun."

"Well, I sent out an A.P.B. to find her and you. I'd rather make you as Momo's killer. You could be facing the gas chamber, even for offing a creep like that. You better turn yourself in."

"Maybe we can cut a deal. Maybe whoever murdered Momo was the guy shooting at me just now. I didn't kill Momo, believe me. And it wasn't Dorie shooting at me. Give me until the morning and I'll tie the whole thing up in a neat package for you. And throw in the identity of the Man."

"Too late. I won't call off the watchdogs. I want you in a cell. Tonight."

The phone clicked off.

18

There's only one place Dorie could be. She must have gone back to his apartment. Had Momo come on to her one time too many? Had she killed him? Or had Dummy? How did she get away? He better call her to warn her to stay low.

He hadn't left the phone booth. He fished around in his pockets for another coin and rang his number. The phone rang and rang. No one picked up. Then, finally, a hesitant voice, hers, asked, "Hello?"

"Are you okay?"

Pause. "Yes."

"Was it you who called the cops? Do you know

who killed Momo?"

"No, it happened while I was in the bathroom, geezing. Momo came home a few minutes earlier and was very nervous. He said the cops had taken him for questioning, but oddly, had never searched him, despite the felony load he was carrying. He didn't understand what was going on, but thought you might have had something to do with it. He was freaking and making me very nervous. I had to have a shot. I was just nodding off in the john when I heard two shots. I locked the bathroom door. When I came out, Momo was lying in a pool of blood. He was dead. I thought maybe you were the killer, dissolving your partnership. Momo wouldn't open the door for anybody, just you or Dummy."

"Listen, babe. I'm a two-bit hustler, con artist, junkie. I've never fired a gun in my life."

"Don't you have a gun? I saw one in your hand the night I dropped in on you."

"That's purely for protection. If junkies know you're carrying shit, you're a prime target, but I'm no gunman."

"Well, you better learn to use your gun – fast. Whoever offed Momo may be coming after you next."

"I'm very aware of the danger. That's why I'm calling. It's time for us to get out of town. Give me an hour. I'll come by with my car. I'll blow the horn twice. Come down fast. Leave everything except my shit and kit and some dough I have stashed. You'll find it all under the sink. It's on a little shelf attached to the bottom. Remember, I'll honk twice. If you're not down in two minutes, I'm leaving you on your own."

"Thanks a lot." And she hung up.

Having made his decision, he was calm. The tension of the last few days was gone; everything was over. The play had failed, but there would be others. He'd learned the game from other failures. In fact, his misgivings were so slight that he wondered why he didn't feel more relief. He grunted and shook his head. His life was still in danger, but he'd managed to disappear before. He wondered where Dummy was. He and the shooter were still around. His station wagon was hidden but might be a hot spot. He was safe for a while, if he could dodge the cops. He almost laughed at the idea that both the good guys and the bad guys wanted him dead. He found a hidden spot down the block from his car. He could watch it for a while to see if the shooter was around.

Might as well geeze while I wait, he thought, digging one of the ounce packages out of a pocket. He carefully opened the tinfoil, laying it flat. He wet the tip of one of his fingers, dipped it in the white powder, and lifted it to his gums and his nose. He sniffed deep and sharp, drawing the heroin into his nose, then repeated the process. It was slower than the needle and wasteful, but his end was achieved. The glow began to creep up. Five minutes later, the hard, damp earth was as comfortable as a downy mattress. It was weird how swift his own reaction had been to the dark figure when the automobile backfired, the result of conditioning. He knew gunfire when he heard it.

Dummy was forgotten as he slipped into euphoria.

Discomfort, fog, death – nothing managed to touch him. He could have entered the gas chamber without trembling; his fear would be sugar-coated by a sense of unreality. It seemed unbelievable that only an hour before he had been stricken with such terror that his mind refused to act. His body went on automatic defense.

Later, he roused himself. The luminous steel hands of his wristwatch pointed to five o'clock. It was beginning to get light – time to get Dorie.

Cautiously, yet without fear, he climbed on one of the metal trash barrels and peered over the fence. The alley was deserted. With a creak of protesting wood, he swung over the fence and dropped, landing in a crouch and not moving, eyes and ears directed to any sound or movement. There was only the faint whirr of an automobile on another street, somewhere in the fog.

His stride was swift and silent. At the first street he waited a long time in the shadows. Then he bolted across the open area and back into the alley blackness. Ahead, through the fog, could be seen the flash of lights from the main boulevard. Like a horse sensing water or home, he quickened his pace. In a few moments he was in his car, heading toward the apartment.

In the fog, the headlights of approaching vehicles on the highway were yellowed and lifeless. The foaming surf of the adjacent beach was no more than a sound in the grayness. He drove slowly, still in happy land. This was no time to get stoned. He was too vulnerable – and too stupid. He swore he'd get off the junk. Tomorrow.

Finally, he pulled up across the street from the front of his apartment building. He thought of Dorie waiting for him, probably half sick for the need of him. She probably had geezed as soon as he told her where he hid his stash. Not a smart move. He blew the horn twice and waited.

Five minutes went by.

He blew the horn twice, again.

No Dorie.

He got out of the car and looked up to the windows of his apartment. Dorie was there. She was signaling him to come upstairs. What the fuck? Why didn't she open the window? Why didn't she come downstairs? He decided to drag her down. He didn't want to leave without her. He slipped across the street after making certain that Dummy and the cops were not in sight.

At the wooden stairs he slowed his ascent as something suddenly probed at his consciousness. He realized that his place was dark. It shouldn't be. Was Dorie signaling him to beat it? Was Dummy up there waiting for him? How had he found his pad? The same sense of danger he'd felt when the car backfired near the Panama Club now surged over him. His stomach rolled over.

Thoughts came at him with stark clarity. His first urge was to turn and run, but he crept up the remaining stairs. He felt certain that Dorie was not alone. Dummy or the other shooter must have had instructions to murder both him and Momo. If that was the case, he wouldn't be leaving Dorie alive as a possible witness, even if she knew nothing of Klein.

He wouldn't be able to surprise anyone waiting for him. He sneaked out the .25 automatic and armed it. Took off the safety. He turned off the light in his hallway and waited. If someone was holding Dorie, he'd be holding a gun just waiting for him to open the door and start blasting. Hadn't he seen Humphrey Bogart in a scene just like this? What did he do?

He slipped by the door, went down on his knees, reached around with the door key to unlock the door. He was not in the doorway and stayed low as he turned the knob, giving the door a soft push with his gun.

"Watch out! He's got a gun, and he's behind the door," shouted Dorie from the darkness.

Immediately came two blasts from inside the room. Bullets fragmented the door and hit the hallway wall behind him. Stark returned fire through the door in the direction of the holes. He heard a whimper of pain and then a thud. A body was blocking the door from opening further. The hallway was full of gunsmoke.

"Dorie, are you OK?"

There was no answer. He had to take a chance and push the door open. "Dorie, are you OK?"

"Yeah, but Dummy looks dead."

He pushed the door open, but Dummy's body lay across the threshold.

"Help me move his body. We got to amscray before the heat arrives in droves. They'll be coming fast and in numbers."

He turned Dummy's body over. Both of his bullets had

scored hits. Too bad Dummy was working for the wrong team. Klein would have to get herself another boy.

A much shaken Dorie switched on the light.

"What are you doing? Let's get out of here. With my record, the cops will be putting me in the gas chamber as fast as they can. We only have minutes to spare."

He and Dorie rushed down the stairs to his car.

"Where to now, Stark? Or aren't you finished killing for today?"

"Did Dummy hurt you?"

"No, but he must have followed me from Momo's place, hoping I would lead him to you. When he knocked at the door, I thought it had to be you. You told me you'd be here in an hour."

"Well, I had to stay out of sight. But if Dummy followed you here, who was it that took shots at me outside the club? Does Klein have more than one runner?"

"Who's Klein?"

"Klein is the Man. Momo's connection. But he's a she. Would you believe a middle-aged business lady? Some front."

"Well, where are we headed? San Francisco?"

"Yeah, but first I need to make a short stop in La Jolla. I need to collect on a past due debt. You remember to bring my stash and cash?"

As he put the key in the ignition, suddenly the car's two back doors were yanked open. Two dark-skinned Mexicans slipped in behind them each pointing a .45.

"Who the fuck are you guys? Are the cops hiring Mexs these days?"

"We not the cops, señor. Jefe says to bring you in dead or alive. It don't matter whichever. He wants to talk to you. You one lucky hombre. First, he didn't much care. Later, he change his mind."

"So, it was you who shot at me?"

"No, my friend here. You lucky he is bad shot."

Stark realized now that this was the same Mexican he'd met earlier and given samples of the high-grade heroin.

"You good salesman. Jefe don't like competition. He kill competition. Your friend, he told us to look for you at your club – before he died."

"You mean Alfie's dead?"

"Si, señor. One dead gringo. But you shoot good, too. Before we can follow you up the stairs, bang, bang, bang. Somebody dead? Now drive. Vamos!"

Stark pulled away from the curb, thinking maybe he and Dorie wouldn't be going to San Francisco after all.

"How did you find me?"

"I remember your big car. I know you come for it. I call Jefe, and he tell me not to kill you. He want meet your boss. We follow your car. Maybe you live."

"Where we going?"

"We making a little trip to Mejico. You will love it there, señor."

Stark realized that they hadn't frisked him. He still had his pistol. It had only three bullets left. Not enough of a heavy hand against a couple of .45s. He wouldn't mind giving up Klein if it would save his neck and Dorie's. Two guys were dead because of Klein – including poor Dummy. They all took advantage of him. He wondered who would get Dummy's car. It was probably parked around here.

As they drove off, Stark hoped that somebody in his building, hearing the shots, looked out the window and saw the thugs forcing their way into his car. Maybe Crowley would think these guys killed Dummy and kidnapped him and the girl.

"Why are you smiling?" Dorie asked. "What's so funny? Am I going to see a third killing in one day? Am I the fourth? What have you gotten me into, Mr. Big Business Man? Why am I always attracted to losers? And you are the biggest loser I've ever met. I'm going to hook up with Mr. Square next. That is, if I get another chance."

"Stop talking, por favor. Drive south," came a voice from the rear.

The fog had not lifted as the night progressed. If anything, it was thicker. The oncoming lights of cars, headed north, were like fast moving ships that loomed past them out of the gloom.

It would be a long night. Their only chance was a possible road block, but in this fog, a battleship could slip past the cops. What would Bogart do now? he wondered.

19

Two slow, agonizing hours later, they were still on the road.

"We need to stop for gas," Stark announced.

"Okay. Be fast or you dead."

They pulled into a brightly lit gas station. It was like a beacon in the dark fog. A young kid came out with a big smile. Probably something he was supposed to do for the customers. Nobody could be happy on a night like this. He told the kid to fill it up. He desperately needed a fix.

"I got to go to the bathroom."

"Me, too," said Dorie.

She knew what he really wanted.

"My compadre go with you. No funny business, or you dead."

"I wish he'd get another line," said Dorie, flippantly.

They got to the bathrooms, their bodyguard dogging their steps, his gun down at his side, away from the attendant. When Dorie tried to open her door, she turned the knob and said, "It's locked."

"Okay," Stark said, "join me." He opened his door and Dorie slipped inside before she could be stopped.

"I know you've come in to geeze. I need some, too," she said.

"I don't have an outfit. We'll just have to share this one hit." He opened the package, and after wetting the tip, he dipped his little finger in the white powder and started rubbing his gums. He passed her the package for a taste. Meanwhile, there was a loud knocking at the door.

"Quick, do you have any lipstick on you?"

"Why? Are your lips chapped? Are you switching sides?" she asked with a wry smile.

"When did you become such a comic? I want to leave a message on the mirror."

The hammering got louder.

He scribbled a quick note. "Call Lt. Crowley 276-9000. We're being kidnapped to Mex. Stark."

The door gave way and Dorie was pulled out first. A gun was shoved, hard, in his side.

"Vamos."

"That will be six dollars twenty-five," said the kid.

"Can I check your oil? Water? This is the last gas station open before San Diego."

"No. We're fine. Here's the dough. Keep the change," Stark said.

They pulled away, back into the fog. It was getting a little lighter. Dawn was still a couple of hours away. As he got into the car, he'd slipped the gun out of his pocket. It lay on the seat, next to him. He didn't know if he'd have the chance to use it. The taste had set him up; instead of nodding off, he was alert, on edge, ready to go.

They passed San Diego. Dorie had fallen asleep, as had the silent thug in the back. His snoring reverberated through the car. Stark tried to move the rearview mirror so he could see if the guy behind him was awake.

"Why you do that? Fix mirror. Drive. I right behind you. Make move, you dead."

"Great," he thought. A guy with a one track mind. If only there was a way to quickly turn around and plug him while the other guy slept. Not likely. He was no Humphrey Bogart. It was blind luck that he'd been able to hit Dummy through that door.

It was getting lighter, the sun about to rise as they passed through the border without a second look from the guards. They didn't care what you brought into Mexico — even if it was two gringo hostages.

As they drove into Tijuana, the town was fast asleep. The garish neon lights turned off. The dusty streets abandoned to the stray dogs and a couple of drunks sleeping it off in a doorway.

"Turn left at light. Go slow. I tell you when to stop."

They stopped at an open cantina. At a table in the back, a tall, light-skinned Mexican stood up. He was wearing a rumpled white suit, white shoes, open white shirt. He was handsome, with nearly black hair swept back. He strode to the car and stuck his hand out to Stark.

"Welcome to my country, Mr. Stark. So glad you could come on this visit," he said with a smile, his white teeth flashing. But his eyes were cold. He was the kind of guy who would be smiling as he put a couple of bullets in you.

"You speak very good English," said Stark. "Are you American? Chicano?"

"Yes, Mr. Stark. The G.I. Bill paid for two years of college because I fought for your country in Korea."

As Stark slowly got out of the car, ignoring the still outstretched hand, the thugs got out, guns drawn. Fortunately, his own had slid beneath the seat.

"I'm not exactly what you call a voluntary guest, Mr....?"

"I shall just give you my professional name. Pablo." The smile was still there. "Come inside. Out of the sun. I have a business proposition for you." He told the heavies to wait.

"And who is this lovely señorita?"

"Dorie. That's my professional name, too, since we're getting so informal. So chummy."

They followed him into the cantina. With a wave of his hand, someone brought out coffee for the three of them. It was strong and bitter; it braced them both.

"Mr. Stark, I hope we can do business. If not, neither of you will leave Mexico. The choice is up to you."

"Some choice."

"I tasted some of the heroin you gave as free samples to one of my dealers. You think I need a new supplier? That shit is twice as strong as my product. And at half the price. Either that shit is stolen merchandise that hasn't been cut, or your boss is bringing it in from some place like Cambodia. I need to meet with your boss. Excuse me."

Pablo got up and held a brief, whispered conversation with one of their guards. He smiled, again, as he returned to the table. "My colleague tells me that you were involved in a shooting in your apartment. They don't know who was killed. I am curious. Was it you that did the shooting, or the young lady? Who was killed? Maybe you can't go back to the States, after all. Dead or alive."

Stark thought about his answers. He didn't owe Klein a thing. She had Dummy murder Momo and would have had him killed, too. It was too bad he'd had to kill the mute. Violence wasn't his game, but here he was, up to his neck in it.

"Maybe my boss and you can do business," answered Stark, avoiding talk of Dummy's murder. "He's got the product, you have the distribution. As long as neither one of you competes with the other. There's no reason for any more killings. It's not good business. You strike me as a practical businessman, Pablo."

"Don't talk down to me. I'm not stupid," responded Pablo testily. "I'm a lot smarter than you are, junkie. I'll

decide whether we join forces or sever things – perma-
nently. Where is this boss?"

"He runs a travel agency in La Jolla." Stark was keeping Klein's identity a secret. It was one way of staying
alive. "I'll take you to him. He won't talk business unless
I'm there."

"You didn't answer me. Who was killed in your apartment?"

"It was a drug heist. The guy was waiting to rip me off.
Dorie helped me to take him out," he lied.

"Stand up," Pablo demanded. He patted Stark down. No
gun. "What did you kill him with? Where's your gun?"

"I dunno. I must have dropped it on the way out. I ran
with my girlfriend. So do you want to meet my boss?"

"Yeah, but your girlfriend stays here. I don't want you
to get any funny ideas. We'll take your car."

Pablo signaled to his men that he would go with Stark,
alone, to La Jolla. Clearly he didn't trust his own men. A
few words in Spanish were passed. Stark didn't understand
a word, but clearly understood when a .45 automatic was
passed to Pablo.

"Stark, are you leaving me with these animals? I don't
like the look of them. I'd rather they shoot me than fuck
me."

Stark asked Pablo for some woman to keep Dorie on ice
until they returned. Pablo yelled in Spanish to the rear
room of the cantina, and a fat, middle-aged Mex woman
came out, wiping her hands. Clearly the patrón's wife.

Dorie stepped into Stark's outstretched arms. She whispered in his ear. "Get back here safely. Watch yourself with this guy," and then more loudly to Pablo, "Take care of my fella. I've gotten quite used to him."

The two men went back to the car. Stark was still in the driver's seat.

"I need something to keep me going. I've been driving all night. Been shot at by one of your goons and had to kill a thief. It's been a long day and a longer night."

"No fixes, junkie. I need you awake until we meet your boss. Then you'll get a long sleep. Here's a couple of dexies to keep you going."

Stark dry-swallowed the pills, but didn't at all like the bit about the long sleep. He put the car in gear and slowly drove down the dusty street, now alive with people and animals, as they headed back to the border.

As they approached the crossing point, he hoped the border cops would stop them.

"You signal these guys," said Pablo, "and your girl-friend and you will both die. I'm not fucking around." The gun prodded into his side. It made the point.

"Would you please open your trunk," the border guard asked politely, after giving the interior of the car a quick glance. A few minutes later, they were back in the U.S. and on the highway headed north.

"I think I should call my boss to let him know we are coming. I'll tell him you want another sample of his product, to make sure of the quality, but that you are coming to discuss a new distribution deal that will make everyone money."

"What's your angle in all this, Mr. Stark? How do you fit in? As near as I can tell, you are a user of the product, not a seller. Why does your boss trust you? I wouldn't. I don't get it."

"I'm not really hooked. I just geeze once in a while. The Beast from the East is not my real hang up. My first choice is weed."

"Are you telling me that your shit comes from the East?"

"Nah, that's just an expression we use. What about the call?"

"Okay. But I'll be standing in the booth with you. One wrong word, and..."

"Okay, okay. I get the picture."

Stark kept watching for a roadside phone booth. Or the cops. Maybe the gas station jockey had seen the lipstick on the mirror and called Crowley. Miracles do happen. Happen all the time in the movies.

Outside a gas station, he spotted a phone booth. Maybe he could leave another message in the bathroom. He thought not. This guy was no dummy.

It was crowded with the two of them and soon got hot in the narrow phone booth. After putting in the additional change for long distance, he was connected to the travel agency in La Jolla.

"Let me speak to Klein, it's Burdman calling."

A few minutes later, a hesitant Klein came on the phone. "Hello," she asked. "Who is this?"

"Klein. It's Stark. I'm on my way to your office. Should

be there in about an hour. I'm bringing you a guy who will make you rich. I've given him some samples of your merchandise. He's thinking of switching to your brand. He can handle a lot of volume."

Pause.

"Have you heard from Dummy?"

"Yeah, he took care of Momo, but missed me. He had a bad accident. He won't be calling in." He chuckled at the idea. There was no laughter from the other end. "Now, you only have me and my new partner to deal with."

"I told you I wanted to think about it. I'm still not ready to go big time."

"I don't really think you have any choice. It's us or the cops."

"Get here at two o'clock. The office closes at one on Saturdays. I'll be waiting for you both."

The line went dead.

"Stark, your Mr. Klein sounds like a woman. I smell a rat."

"No, no. This is legit. She's a dame. But no sweetheart, believe me. She wants us to show up at two when there will be no witnesses. She's got a staff of kids who work for her. The travel agency is no front. A great cover. The cops would never tumble to it."

As they got back in the car, Stark bent over quickly as if he was putting the key in the ignition and reached under the seat for his gun, sliding it into his left pants pocket as they pulled away. Pablo was watching the road for oncoming cars.

They rode the rest of the way in silence, Stark thinking of how to get out of this jam and free Dorie in Mexico. Nothing came to him. He tried to figure out Pablo, but the guy wouldn't talk. Every time he tried to start up a conversation, to pass the time, he was told to shut up. He turned on the radio, hoping to catch some jazz. Instead, he got the news, which he tried to tune out. Suddenly, he caught his name. The police were looking for an Ernie Stark, white male, in connection with the murder of two men, both suspected of narcotics dealing. There followed a more detailed description.

The A.P.B. must still be out on him. The cops were probably looking for his station wagon. Pablo heard the same report.

"Stark? That's you. Two murders? You must be some tough guy. You're hotter than a firecracker. If they're looking for you, they must be looking for this car. Pull in at the next bus stop you spot. We'll ditch the car and take a bus to La Jolla. After the meeting, you're on your own. You're too hot. You'll draw the cops like flies on sugar cane."

They ditched the car a couple of streets over from the bus stop. They waited an hour for the next bus. The bus was overcrowded with people too poor to own cars. Most of them Mex. The bus stank. Pablo's nice white suit was getting messy, Stark noticed with a smile.

It was after three when, after many stops, they finally rolled into La Jolla, both of them sweaty and dusty. Some businessmen, Stark thought. The agency lights were off.

The sign in the door said "Closed." Stark knocked, loudly, hoping Klein could hear it in the back room. He saw her, finally, come to the glass door. She didn't look happy.

"You're late. Where's your car?"

"We had to ditch it."

"I heard the news that Dummy and Momo are dead. Is that your doing, or his?" pointing to Pablo.

"He didn't do it. Let's get inside where we can talk. This is Mr. Pablo, my associate."

Pablo did not smile or stretch out his hand. As they walked to the rear room, he asked, "Where's Mr. Klein? Stark kept talking about the Man."

"There's no Mr. Klein. Stark knows that. I'm the boss."

Inside her office, Klein sat behind her desk and pointed to the two chairs opposite. "Well, Mr. Pablo, what's your proposition?"

"First, I need to know where your narcotics are coming from. This is high-grade shit, if you'll pardon the vernacular."

"I won't tell you. That's my protection."

Pablo pulled out his .45 and pointed it at her. "Lady, you don't have any protection. If you want to live, you'll answer all my questions."

"It's coming in from Thailand. I have a branch of the agency there. I am sent a package by courier as I need it. The package is marked 'Tourist information,'" said Klein, a little more hesitantly, as she looked down the barrel of the gun.

"Let me check another sample. How do I know the

taste that I got from Stark was not specially created as a sell technique at a special discount price?"

"I can assure you that all of my product is first class and never sold below market." She got up and went to a wall-safe behind a picture of Thailand hanging behind her seat, opened the safe, and took out several packets.

"Try any one you want. You'll see they are all the real McCoy."

Pablo pulled one packet across the desk with his left hand, the gun in his right, still pointing at her. As he tried to crack open the packet with his left thumb, his attention was momentarily distracted. Klein whipped open her desk drawer, but before she could get her gun out, Pablo fired twice. A .45 bullet leaves a big hole. The top of her head flew off and splattered the picture. Blood poured out over the desk and the samples as Klein fell over dead.

"I hate competition," said Pablo. "Especially from amateurs. Especially gringas."

As he began to swivel around his chair, Stark whipped out his .25 and fired three times into the white suit and self-satisfied smile. The room was filled with gun smoke. Good thing the neighboring stores on both sides of the travel agency were also closed this hot Saturday afternoon.

Swiftly, Stark stood and wiped his fingerprints off his gun and put it in Klein's right hand. The cops will think they killed each other, he thought. He picked up her gun. He would need it.

He went to the safe and took nearly every bindle of shit

he could find. There was almost twenty-five ounces there. He'd leave enough for the cops to buy the story of a drug deal gone bad. He'd taken enough to set up his own business in another city. And cash. He didn't count it all, but it looked like twenty-five Gs. He was in business, for real, now. He threw it all into the bank deposit bag he found in the safe.

He needed wheels to get back to Dorie. Remembering that Klein had her car parked out behind the agency, he went through her purse and found the car keys. He took the cash in her wallet, as well. Every bit helped.

Before he left, he made sure to wipe his prints from the chair he'd been sitting in. He reached over the desk and picked up the packet Pablo had been trying to open. He needed a taste just to get back on the road. Klein's blood hadn't soaked the powder. He found the back door and opened it, then wiped down his prints with Klein's handkerchief.

Her car was just where he thought it would be. It was a beauty. A new Cadillac, with a dark blue finish. As he got into the car, he put Klein's gun in the glove compartment. He realized that it was one of his dreams to drive a great new car like this. It made him feel rich. Shit, he was rich. If only he didn't have to go back to Mexico for Dorie. He turned the motor on and thought about it for a moment. He didn't owe her anything. He never wanted anyone to owe him either. She was a survivor. She'd get back on her own.

20

As he nosed the Caddy out on to Main Street, the car, almost as if it knew he'd made up his mind, headed south for the border.

"I must be nuts," he said aloud. Stark was wrestling with himself. "The dame doesn't mean anything to me. All right, she is a knock-out, has a nice sense of humor, has all the right moves in bed, but remember how quickly she wanted to set up house after one night? How did she hook me?

"I'll be goddamned. Me, whose philosophy is to always keep moving. Never get tied down. Never let a dame get her hooks into you. The con artist conned by a dame.

You'd never see Humphrey Bogart take a fall for some skirt. Didn't he even send his girlfriend to prison?"

How was he going to free Dorie, surrounded by Pablo's goons? They'd not be happy to see him – without their boss. Maybe he could buy them off with this Caddy? Must be worth a fortune in Mexico. Nah, that wouldn't work. Not the dough or the high grade shit he was going to use to set up his own business would buy Dorie free.

The Caddy kept heading south. Always within the speed limit. Crowley must have discovered his abandoned station wagon by now. Would it confuse him that the car was headed north when Stark parked it? Or would Crowley think that he and Dorie had hoofed it into Mexico? Whatever, he'd have every badge in the state looking for him.

Maybe he should give the copper a call. They wouldn't find Klein's and Pablo's bodies until Monday morning when the agency opened for business. Maybe he should give Crowley the news and let him wrap the whole business up. He wanted the Man. The Dealer. He'd give him two. And Momo's murderer. Maybe that would buy him off.

He pulled into the first gas station on the road with a phone booth. It wasn't until he told the gas jockey to fill it up that he realized this was the same gas station he'd stopped in last night with the hoods. Fortunately, it was a different jockey. He checked the men's room. His lipstick message was still there. Under it was another message: "Call Kilroy instead."

After feeding enough coins into the phone to satisfy the

long distance operator, he was put through to Crowley. "Where are you? You are dead meat unless you turn yourself in. I've got the whole L.A.P.D. looking for you."

"Let me get a word in, for Christ's sake."

"No, you listen to me. Not only are you wanted for Momo's murder, but we found Dummy's body. And guess whose apartment he was found shot in? Yours, bright boy. We're talking a double homicide. It's the gas chamber, unless you come in. Even then I can't guarantee to save your ass."

"Listen carefully, Crowley. I'm not coming in. I'm not going to take the frame for both murders. Check Dummy's gun. You'll see he fired the bullets that killed Momo. He was gunning for me. Waiting in my own apartment to take me down. I shot him first, but this was home invasion. He's a killer, and I was next on his list.".

"Tell it to the judge. You are not conning me, kid. I'm making you for both murders."

"Crowley, I'm no patsy. I'll trade you two more stiffs for a long leash."

"Long leash? Are you kidding? What could you possibly trade that would get you off the hook?"

"Two top drug dealers. You've been after me to find out who Momo's supplier is. The Man. Well, the Man is not a man. It's a middle-aged woman. A legitimate business person who's been supplying Momo."

"Give me a name."

"Not so fast. I can also turn over the boss who's been running the Mex network. He's an even bigger deal."

"How do I know you're telling the truth?"

"I was there when the two dealers shot it out. No on
has found their bodies, yet. There's drugs and records i
her safe. The guy probably has a record."

"Sounds fishy to me."

"Her staff will identify me as Mr. Burdman. I met he
a couple of days ago. Dummy left me a clue that I fol
lowed up."

"So where can I find these individuals?"

He gave Crowley the address of the travel agency.

"La Jolla? That's out of my jurisdiction. That's no
going to do me any good."

"Crowley, call the head of the California Narcotic
Squad. Tip him off that one of your 'agents' uncovered
both ringleaders. They'll give you a promotion."

"Let's see how things play out. Meanwhile, call m
back tomorrow. I'll call off the bloodhounds for twenty
four hours until I see if this story is legit. It better be."

"What a pal," said Stark as the phone disconnected.

It was late afternoon as Stark neared the border. He wa:
tired and a little strung out. He needed to fix or at leas
get another taste to keep going. He still hadn't figured ou
how he was going to rescue Dorie. Some suicide mission.

As his car pulled into the long line of vehicles, mostly
American guys looking for a hot, cheap Saturday night in
Tijuana, he noticed, on the other side of the road, a dame
hitchhiking. Her thumb stuck out, her dress hiked up.
Showing some leg to the sucker who might pick her up.
But all the traffic was heading south.

It took him a moment to register that the dame was Dorie. How the fuck had she managed to escape? Was he seeing things? He made a fast U-turn and pulled up alongside her.

"Nice car," she said coolly. "Did you just buy it? Looks new."

"Nah. It's a trade-in. I got a good price on the station wagon. The dealer said it's a valuable antique. Looking for a ride?"

"I'd rather go with anyone else, but it looks like you're the only choice," she quipped.

"How'd you escape? There were two mugs watching you."

Dorie got in the car. "Fortunately, there's a thing here called siesta. The two gentlemen were acting like rapists, so the Mrs. Cantina locked me in a back room and stood guard. I fell asleep, and when I woke up, she was snoring. I opened the latch on the door with my bobby pin. It wasn't a real lock, just a hook-up job. The two heavies were asleep on tables in the cantina, so I just tip-toed out. I didn't think they'd come after me if I tried to hitch a ride from the American side and close to the border cops."

"Smooth. No muss. No fuss. And, we're away."

"What happened to Pablo?"

"The same thing he was planning for me. I just moved a minute faster. Faster than Klein did. He took her out and almost made it a double."

"So now what do we do? Won't the cops be after us? Actually, it's you they want. Not me. I was just going along for the ride. Nice, though, to think that you were coming to my rescue. I never thought I'd see you again. Dead or alive."

As Stark steered the car north, he decided to share his luck with Dorie.

"Look what goodies I've brought you, babe. Look at this stash I copped from Klein's safe. There's enough here to get stoned for a couple of years and enough cash for us to go into business. Even legit."

He showed her the bag with the bindles and the cash.

"Are you nuts? Every cop in California is looking for you. And you want to go into the drug business? Pull over," she said. "I need to get a taste. I'm really strung out."

Stark pulled over to the side of the road. He needed to piss. He stepped down into the ditch at the side of the road to be out of sight of passing cars. As he did so, he heard the Caddy pull away. Dorie was driving off. The hustler had been out-hustled.

As the Caddy disappeared up the road, Stark smiled to himself. He hadn't told Dorie that the Caddy was Mrs. Klein's. The cops would soon be looking for it. He'd also forgotten to tell her that Klein's gun was in the glove compartment. Or that he'd kept half of the dough in his pants pocket.

About a quarter mile down the road, the Caddy pulled over. Had she changed her mind? Stark hustled after her. As he came up to the car, the bank bag was thrown to the side of the road. In it looked like half the cash and half the bindles. The dame had a heart.

He didn't have enough to start a new business, but he had twenty-four hours and dough that would get him to Canada and out of Crowley's reach. There's a whole new market for suckers in Canada awaiting a smooth con man like himself. He whistled as he walked along the road, ready for new action and a new scene.

THE END

Afterword

I was completely taken aback when Nat Sobel, Eddie's book agent, asked me to write this brief background to Eddie's last (and first) novel. I protested that he should write it. After all, wasn't he (like a modern times Maxwell Perkins) the one who resurrected it? Calling me to see what unfinished work remained, locating the manuscript in a publisher's office outside of London, stitching it together, finding a new publisher? He disagreed. And after thinking about it, I suppose he's right in that, perhaps, I am the only one that could know the details surrounding *Stark*.

My relationship with Eddie spanned thirty years.

Prison, halfway house counselor, wife for twenty years, mother of his son, and always his close friend. It would be safe to say that I heard all of his "stories." As he wrote in a letter to me in 1996, "My beloved and best friend... if my life is adjudged a plus, it is because I have my private angel to give me a haven and at least enough peace to work." I write this, then, as the "beloved and best friend" of the not-so distant past; and as the mother of his son. It's really an honor – to once again assist in whatever way so that his work can be brought to life again.

Imagine someone with a seventh-grade education wanting to be a serious writer? He had no guidance. He had to teach himself everything. The prison psychologist said it was another "manifestation of infantile fantasy." His gift was an above average I.Q.; and from the age of seven, he was a voracious reader. He discovered that he could see the world through endless different eyes and minds, could experience life in Ancient Egypt, modern India, the Middle Ages. He thought most Americans didn't value books. He thought that in America, only money mattered; and that although money was necessary for everything, to read widely is to have more of Life itself.

His parents divorced when he was four, and he was made a ward of the court at seven years of age. A child abandoned to the wilderness adopts its ways. Read his third novel, *Little Boy Blue*, for more on that. His childhood was a war with the world, and he burned through reform schools, escaping at every chance. He'd been adopted for a short period by Louise Fazenda Wallis, his benefactress, when he was fourteen or fifteen years old. At seventeen, he was the youngest inmate to ever enter San Quentin. It was 1950 (one year before I was born). For a brief time he had back to back cells with Caryl Chessman (Chessman was on death row; on the opposite side, Eddie was not). They spoke through the ventilator pipes about literature. One day a convict surreptitiously brought him a folded magazine under a hand towel and handed it to him through the bars. He opened it up. It was a copy of *Argosy* magazine. On the cover, the lead piece was "Cell 2455, Death Row by Caryl Chessman." A light bulb exploded. He couldn't believe it! Writers went to Harvard or Yale or Princeton. Chessman had also been raised by the State. If Chessman could write a bestseller, then why couldn't he?

The idea was so sudden and intense that he couldn't sleep. He wrote his benefactress, and she sent him a type-writer – a secondhand, Royal Aristocrat, and a subscription to the *Sunday New York Times* Book Review. The reviews talked about Thomas Wolfe, John Dos Passos, F. Scott Fitzgerald, Faulkner, Hemingway, Dreiser, Jack London, Dostoevsky, William Styron, and others. He studied *The Elements of Style*, by E.B. White; and culled his memory for all the tales and crime stories he'd seen from his unique perspective. His research was his life as he lived it.

This brings us to *Stark*. By this time, he's around thirty-three years of age. The year is 1963. He's a four-time loser. His typewriter had, by then, bit the dust. No matter. He had access to typewriters and paper. He wrote in long hand first, with a pencil. He had two prison jobs. The first was as the head lieutenant's secretary. He was responsible for writing and typing all reports on "incidents" within the prison, so that they could be sent to Sacramento as required. His other job was in the prison library. It was there that he educated himself about the law. Every convict with a legal question would come to him. It got so he couldn't go out on the yard, because he'd get "mobbed." He'd also gotten to know lawyers who could take his pages out, though he had to sell his blood in prison to pay the postage for sending them to publishers. He still had his dreams, but he wondered if they would really ever see the light of day.

He described *Stark* as a story about a con man. Eddie didn't think much of con men, because, as a rule, they preyed upon people weaker than themselves. But he understood them. He thought it was worth telling a story from such a character's point of view. He once told our son: "We are what we have been taught to be by many influences. No more, no less. Remember that because it will instill humility instead of arrogant self-righteousness."

He had a chance to look at the underbelly of life from a unique position. He never tried to impose a preconception, or ignore or twist a fact to make any position more persuasive. He was obsessed with the "Truth," and with finding it. He always said he was as dedicated to the Truth as a prelate to the Church. It was ironic: he was an atheist, but aspired to the Transcendent. "If there is a rule we should follow, it is to seek truth as best we can, via whatever paths we can find." What he most wanted was a chance to last, a lotus to grow from the mud.

Jennifer Steele

Edward Bunker titles can be obtained from

NO EXIT PRESS

978-1-84243-264-8	Stark	£6.99
978-1-84243-266-2	No Beast So Fierce NE	£7.99
978-1-84243-267-9	Animal Factory NE	£7.99
978-1-84243-268-6	Little Boy Blue NE	£7.99
978-1-84243-269-3	Dog Eat Dog NE	£7.99
978-1-84243-270-0	Mr Blue NE	£9.99

Please send orders to;

HIGH STAKES BOOKSHOP
21 Great Ormond Street,
London WC1N 3JB

Add fifteen per cent P&P. Cheques payable to High Stakes in Sterling drawn on UK bank or pay by credit card (Visa, MasterCard, Maestro) quoting card number, expiry date, 3 digit security code and valid from date and issue number where appropriate

Tel 020 7430 1021
Fax 020 7430 0021

Or order online at www.noexit.co.uk/bunker